The Universes Inside *the* Lighthouse

a Balky Point adventure

D0006054

Pam Stucky

Published in the United States by Wishing Rock Press.

Cover design and artwork by Jim Tierney jimtierneyart.com
Illustrations by Ken Schrag and Yasuko Nakamura

ISBN: 1940800072 (print)
ISBN-13: 978-1-940800-07-3 (print)
eBook ISBN-13: 978-1-940800-08-0
eBook ISBN: 1940800080

www.wishingrockpress.com

the Universes Inside the Lighthouse

a Balky Point adventure

Books by Pam Stucky

FICTION

The Balky Point Adventures (Middle Grade/YA sci-fi)
The Universes Inside the Lighthouse
The Secret of the Dark Galaxy Stone
The Planet of the Memory Thieves

Mystery
Death at Glacier Lake
Final Chapter (A Megan Montaigne Mystery)

The Wishing Rock series (contemporary fiction) (novels with recipes)
Letters from Wishing Rock
The Wishing Rock Theory of Life
The Tides of Wishing Rock

NONFICTION

the Pam on the Map travel series
Iceland
Seattle Day Trips
Retrospective: Switzerland
Retrospective: Ireland

From the Wishing Rock Kitchens: Recipes from the Series

www.pamstucky.com
twitter.com/pamstucky
facebook.com/pamstuckyauthor
pinterest.com/pamstucky

for Dean and Paula
whose lives I hope are full of an abundance of
spectacular adventures

the universes await ...

Discover all of the Balky Point Adventures!

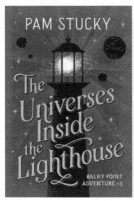

The Universes Inside the Lighthouse
The Secret of the Dark Galaxy Stone
The Planet of the Memory Thieves

chapter one

"There! Left of the moon. Over those tall trees. Did you see it?"

Emma Nelson readjusted the multitude of pillows cushioning her body from the hard, bumpy back of the truck's cab. She and her twin brother, Charlie, had been sitting in the bed of the pickup for two hours already, having arrived at this prime sky-viewing spot just before sunset. Emma tracked her gaze along the direction of the dark shadow of Charlie's arm as he pointed up into the night sky.

"I missed it again," she replied, wrapping her plum-colored sleeping bag more tightly around her shoulders. Even on this early August evening, the night came with a bit of a chill. "What did it look like?"

"Like the sky was shifting," said Charlie, lying back down on the air mattress beneath them. "Shimmery. Like looking at the sky through water after someone's thrown a rock in the lake."

"Missed it," repeated Emma. She scooted to lie down again next to her brother, slipping into her sleeping bag.

"Maybe if you'd stop fidgeting," said Charlie.

Emma didn't reply. She couldn't help it if she was fidgety. Her mind wasn't on the sky.

The twins fell silent again, watching.

Two weeks earlier, their family had arrived back on Dogwinkle

Island, a small island more or less near Seattle, for a summer vacation "away from it all"—or at least, that's how their mom and dad had put it. Their parents had dragged them out to the island over Christmas break to scout out this island as a possible vacation spot. The teens had not been terribly excited about the idea at first, but then Emma had met a friendly local boy and her opinion had changed. After that she'd been eager to get back, but on their return she'd learned the young man, Ben, was away. Emma and Charlie had been amusing themselves as best they could on this remote island. A week-long "Dogwinkle Days" festival and parade had provided entertainment for a while, but with the event over, the twins were bored again. Ed Brooks, the man from whom their family had rented a vacation cabin, had suggested they try this camping spot, a broad and wide clearing in the deeply forested northern part of the island.

"We saw UFOs there once," Ed had told them.

"Or maybe it was northern lights," his new wife, Ruby, had added, the tone of her voice rich with the rolling of eyes.

Whether UFOs or northern lights, any diversion was welcome. So far, they hadn't been disappointed. At least Charlie (the younger by half an hour) hadn't. Emma seemed to blink at all the wrong times, look left when the action was right, look down the second the sky lit up.

Emma was a homebody, in all senses of the word. She liked home and all its comforts. She did not like bugs, or sleeping on the ground, or the idea of being mauled by bears or stray wild boars or whatever nefarious indigenous monsters the island might be hiding. On hearing this, in his great kindness, Ed Brooks had loaned the teens his truck with its extended cab and extended bed, normally used for deliveries from his whiskey distillery. He'd asked if they wanted an enclosed van. Emma had wanted to say yes, but had been too embarrassed to admit it.

"Drive it carefully," Ed had admonished, patting the white truck lovingly on the side. "You have a license, right?"

Charlie had puffed up. "We've been driving for a year, thanks."

Ed had laughed, handed over the keys.

Charlie shifted in the bed of the truck so he was facing Emma, even though they could barely see each other in the dark. "Did you hear Ben is back?"

Emma was glad for the cover of night, as she felt the blood rising to her face. Anyone else might not have heard the mocking smile in his tone, but she did. "He is?" she said, trying to be nonchalant, but it was pointless. Charlie knew her as well as she knew herself, and vice versa.

"He is indeed," Charlie said, his amusement clear. He loved his sister, but he loved teasing her, too. "Ed told Dad that Ben and his brother were off in Iceland for a few weeks. That's where they've been. They just got back today."

"Hm," said Emma, but her mind whirred. Iceland! She had not heard that part. An adventurer, then! Her attention wandered from the sky again as she imagined herself and Ben cuddling together in an igloo. Did they have igloos in Iceland? She was going to have to do some research. Looking like an ignorant idiot in front of Ben was not an option. Maybe they'd get married in Iceland. Everyone could fly—

"There!" Charlie cried out. "Did you see that one?"

Emma looked up, too late, again. "Missed it," she sighed.

Charlie laughed lightly. "More moon, less mooning, Em." His voice softened. "We'll go find him tomorrow so you can just accidentally run into him. But pay attention to the sky tonight. We need to catch some UFOs!"

"Tomorrow," she said, "after I shower. This sleeping bag is terrible. I'm cold but I'm also sweating. I feel so gross." She punched Charlie in the arm. "Dork."

Charlie punched her back lightly. "Dork."

And then they focused on the stars.

Just in time, as a blazing white-yellow light appeared out of nowhere, streaked brightly across half the sky directly overhead, and disappeared as fast as it had appeared.

The forest went silent.

"What was that?" said Emma, exhaling. She realized she'd been holding her breath.

"An airplane?" said Charlie, skeptically.

"Could be," said Emma, though she didn't really believe it either. "But where did it come from? And where did it go?"

Neither of them had an answer.

Once she'd settled into the night and let go of thoughts about her own honeymoon with Ben, Emma, too, had seen a lot of action in the sky. Her luck continued the next day: when she and Charlie drove down to Wishing Rock to return Ed's truck, Emma was surprised and delighted, and perhaps a bit anxious, to find Ed sitting at a picnic table out front of the town building—visiting with Ben, the one heavenly body she most wanted to see. Wishing Rock was the small community at the southern tip of the island where Ed and Ben lived. In the unusual community, everyone in town lived in the same large, refurbished, L-shaped building. The town had been built a few decades earlier by Ed's grandfather.

"Children!" called out Ed, waving at Emma and Charlie to come join them. "You brought back my truck in one piece, I hope?"

"Not a scratch!" said Charlie, shaking Ed's hand as he returned the truck keys. "Better than you left it!"

Ed and Ben were sitting on opposite sides of the picnic table.

Charlie slipped onto the bench next to Ed, leaving the seat next to Ben open for Emma. She was grateful for what she knew was conscious effort on her brother's part, but felt a blush rise up from the back of her neck.

"Hi, Emma," said Ben with a warm smile. "Hey, Charlie!" The young men reached across and fist-bumped each other.

Such ease of existence in the world, Emma thought. Being a teen boy seemed so much easier than being a teen girl. She smiled shyly back at the handsome young man. "Hey, Ben." *Smooth*, she thought.

"Ben!" said Charlie. "Great to see you again!"

Ed reached across the table to give Emma's hand a welcoming grasp. "Great camping spot, am I right? I gotta get up there again myself." Ed looked at Ben. "I sent them up to that spot where your dad and I saw the UFOs that time." He turned his attention back to Emma and Charlie. "One of these days someone is going to prove us right. I'm certain we saw something supernatural. No one believes us, but I feel it in my gut. So, what about you guys? Did you see anything unusual?"

Emma focused on Ed to calm herself. "Definitely," she nodded. The strange activity from the night before, combined with nervous energy on seeing Ben, left her chattering. Normally she was quiet in groups, listening more than speaking, but she liked Ed, and she liked this island. She felt comfortable in this place in a way she never did at home or at school with her peers, whom she just couldn't quite understand. She never fit in at home. But there was something about this place that made her feel like she belonged. "It's like you said. The shimmery sky, mostly, is what we saw. A couple times—"

"—there was definitely something not normal," Charlie, the more gregarious and outgoing of the two, finished her sentence eagerly. "Could have been planes, except they appeared and disappeared. Out of nowhere, into nowhere. Weird. Awesome."

"Totally what we saw when we were out there," said Ed. "Right, Ben?" He tipped his head toward the dark-haired young man. "Ben's heard the stories a time or two."

"Or fifty," Ben said. "Yeah. Shimmers. Lights. That's the way they tell it." Ben's smile at Emma indicated he wasn't so sure his dad and Ed weren't full of it.

His gaze was overpowering. Emma had to remind herself to breathe. "Have you ever seen it yourself, Ben?" she asked, quietly.

Charlie, both a pain in the behind to his sister and also her biggest fan, recognized her struggle. "Yeah, Ben, you should come along with us next time! Want to go? Maybe I'll ask that girl I saw at the parade to come along." He pulled out his phone and brought up his pictures. Much to his delight, he'd managed to get a picture of the attractive young stranger without being too obvious. "Do you know this girl? I don't remember seeing her when we were in Wishing Rock in December."

While Emma tried to will herself not to blush furiously at Charlie's suggestion that Ben join them, Charlie passed the phone to Ben, who scrutinized the picture with enthusiasm. "No," he said, raising his eyebrows, "I think I'd remember her."

"She's not local?" asked Charlie.

"Never seen her before," said Ben. "But now I'm curious."

Emma's heart sank.

"Your mystery dream girl," said Emma.

"She's not from Wishing Rock, and I don't think I've ever seen her at Moon Bay, either," said Ed, referring to the second of the island's three small towns. "Maybe she's from Balky Point?"

"That's the town with the lighthouse?" asked Emma.

"Our camping spot was near there, though, wasn't it, Ed?"

asked Charlie.

"Yes and yes," said Ed. "You weren't too far from it last night."

Ben leaned toward Emma. "Some people say the lighthouse is haunted," he said, a sparkle in his eye.

"Haunted!" she said, her nervousness suddenly disappearing. This was what she liked about Ben: even in her extreme discomfort at being around him in all his fabulousness, he made her comfortable, made her forget how anxious she was around him. Like Charlie, he was easygoing, comfortable in his own skin. Confident. Like her, though, he seemed to listen more than talk. She envied that balance.

Ed nodded. "Haunted. Strange things happen there sometimes, I've heard. Never seen it myself. Balky Point is a pretty small community, only about fifty people there, I think. Maybe they're just trying to drive business up there, who knows."

"Can we get into the lighthouse?" Charlie continued, eager for a new place to explore. The idea of a haunted lighthouse was compelling.

"As far as I know, it's usually unlocked," said Ed. "Worth a look, anyway. It's a nice lighthouse, as lighthouses go, I suppose."

Emma and Charlie exchanged a look: tomorrow, to the lighthouse.

Unable to contain their anticipation, Emma and Charlie biked from the cabin out to the lighthouse right after breakfast the next morning. The day was warm, the sun high in the sky: a perfect day to be outside. When they got to the lighthouse, Charlie was distracted by a long set of stairs next to the building leading down to the beach, the gentle waves sparkling in the sunshine. The lighthouse would wait a few more minutes. He jumped off his bike and ran down the steps before Emma could even get off her bike. She followed him, carefully picking her way down the weathered steps.

Charlie skipped rocks while Emma alternated between staring up at the red-and-white-striped lighthouse and scanning the rocky beach for any special stones that might catch her eye. Ed had told them how Wishing Rock got its name, and she was on the lookout to find a nice one for herself.

"My grandfather was originally going to call our town Inaboks—a town in a box—but luckily some people brought him to his senses before that happened. Instead, he named the town after wishing rocks. They're all over our beaches. They're the rocks with a white stripe, a white ring around them. Those are wishing rocks. Make a wish on one, and it'll come true," Ed had promised with a grand smile.

Emma had laughed. She liked Ed. "Exactly how long does it take for the wish to come true?" she asked.

"You know, Emma," Ed had said, "time is a funny funny thing. Still, it never hurts to wish."

Emma agreed. She had a very important wish she needed to make, and it involved a handsome dark-haired eighteen-year-old whose name began with B. It felt like Ben had expressed more interest in a picture of a girl on a phone than in real-life, right-there Emma, and who could blame him? The girl was beautiful. Regardless of whether wishes on wishing rocks worked, Emma could use all the help she could get.

Sensing her mood, Charlie called out to his sister as he lobbed stones into the water. "If he doesn't like you, he's stupid, you know."

"I know," she said. She knew. Still.

A bright white stone about three feet from her left toe caught her eye and interrupted her self-pity. "What is that?" she wondered out loud. Her class had studied rocks in fifth grade geology. She remembered igneous, sedimentary, and metamorphic. She remembered obsidian, limestone, pumice, marble, slate, and shale. But this, she could not place. She didn't remember any stones as bright and smooth and shining and white as this, glowing as though it had energy inside it, burning to get out.

"What is this?" she called out, louder, as she bent to pick up the rock. She held it up high for Charlie to see. "I can't remember what kind of rock this is."

Charlie tossed his remaining handful of rocks into the surf and went to his sister's side. Emma passed the smooth stone to him.

"I don't remember, either," he said, just as Emma had expected. Charlie was smart, but in school he was more interested in making people laugh than in studying geology. He handed the rock back to his sister and hopped across the beach back to the waves.

Emma pulled a bottle of water out of her backpack and took a drink as she watched Charlie, so carefree. How did he end up so easygoing, when her mind was always racing? But even as she thought it, she knew it wasn't true. He was a much deeper thinker than people gave him credit for.

The August sun dazzled off the water. Emma squinted and blinked, thinking she saw trails of light following Charlie as he walked. She put the water bottle back in her pack, along with the white rock, then rubbed her eyes. The trails were gone. "Must remember to drink more water," she said to herself.

A spider ran across the rocks at Emma's feet, and she shuddered. They'd been down at the beach for a good while already, and she was eager to see the lighthouse. Besides which: bugs. "Charlie!" she called out again. When he turned, she pointed at the cliffs. "Let's go back up."

When they'd run down the stairs earlier they'd noticed there were a lot of steps, but going up made that fact crystal clear. "... One hundred seventy-seven, one hundred seventy-eight ... good stars ...

One. Hundred. Seventy-nine. One hundred and seventy-nine steps, my dear sister," said Charlie, panting and puffing. "What this cliff needs is a good elevator. Make note of that, please, to tell the committee."

Since they were little, Charlie and Emma had always told each other to "make note of that, please, to tell the committee." How it started, who the committee was, and what they had ever thought the committee would do about it, neither could remember. But telling each other to make note of that, please, to tell the committee was as familiar to them now as breathing, an automatic response, like saying "Gesundheit!" when the other sneezed.

"Noted," said Emma, catching her breath behind him. "Looks empty," she said as she approached the lighthouse. Could it really be haunted? She knocked on the entrance door. "Hello?" she said, pushing the door open. As Ed had predicted, it was unlocked. "Hello?" she repeated, stepping into the cool, dim room. "Anyone here?" She didn't believe in ghosts, not really. But she did not particularly want to be proven wrong today.

Charlie followed her inside. "I think it's empty," he confirmed, "but it feels …"

"… not empty," Emma finished. Despite there being no signs of life, there was an energy to the air, an electricity, like in the millisecond just before you get a static shock from clothes fresh out of the dryer in the depths of a cold winter. An air of possibility, of something about to happen. Emma shuddered.

The entrance room was small, maybe ten by fifteen feet, with an opening off to the side that led to a circular stairwell, which curved up to the top of the lighthouse. A few rustic and timeworn forest green benches lined the edges of the room. A small Plexiglas-topped table in the center of the room protected a display map of the land masses around Balky Point that could be seen from the lighthouse. Faded old pictures hung on the walls.

"I'm going up!" called out Charlie, the words trailing behind him as he raced up the circular stairway as though he hadn't just climbed one hundred and seventy-nine steps from the beach.

Emma stayed below scanning the photos on the walls, mostly of groups of people smiling cheerily into the camera. The pictures were labeled: "Balky Point, 1900." "Balky Point, 1911." "Balky Point, 1918."

"Must be the town residents?" Emma pondered out loud.

She casually glanced at the first few, but then a chill spread up her spine. She studied the photos more closely. Was that …? She looked at the next photo in line. And that …? But it can't be!

"Charlie! Come here!" she yelled in the direction of the staircase.

Charlie either didn't hear or was not interested in coming back just yet.

"Charlie!" Emma repeated, loudly. "Charlie, come down here!"

This time, Charlie clomped gracelessly but quickly down the stairs. "What? Em! Are you okay? What happened?"

Breathless, he raced to stand by her side.

She was staring at the wall.

Charlie looked at the wall.

"Neat wall," he said, glancing at Emma out of the corner of his eye. "Great wall, Emma."

She said nothing.

They stared at the wall.

Finally, Charlie whispered, "What are we looking at that was so important?"

Emma reached out to touch the glass on the picture in front of her. "This girl," she said, pointing to a girl in the background of the picture, not part of the posed group, but separate, apart. She moved her finger. "And this man, beside her."

"Huh," said Charlie. "That girl looks a lot like—"

Emma, who had moved on to the next picture, interrupted him. "A lot like this girl," she said, again pointing to a young woman who again was in the background of the picture, almost hiding, but not quite. "And this man."

She moved to another picture. "And this girl, and this man."

Charlie's mouth gaped open. "But that's …"

"Show me your phone," she said.

Charlie, who already knew what Emma was thinking, had his phone out and was scrolling through his photos. He found the one he was looking for, held it up to the wall next to the girl in the picture, the girl in all the pictures. 1900. 1918. 1929. The same girl, the same age, in every picture. And in his phone.

The girl from the Dogwinkle Days Parade.

"That's totally her," he said. "But … how?"

Emma pursed her lips. How, indeed? She looked again from one picture to the next. Could it be a younger sister, daughter, different generations through the years? Of course it was possible—everything was possible—but her gut told her this was the same person. The man's picture was blurrier in most of the shots, as though he'd been moving fast when the pictures were taken, making it harder to tell if he was the same person throughout. But Emma's instinct told her it was.

Without looking at Charlie, she said, "We should ask Ben. Maybe he knows."

Charlie laughed. "You just want an excuse to see Ben," he said. "Can't fool me, Emma-bo-bemma."

"Well, so what if I do," she huffed. "You just want to see this girl, and you don't even know her."

Charlie was not deterred. "Can't fool me, Emma-bo-bemma, can't fool Charlie-bo-barley!" he repeated in a sing-song.

"Can't fool a fool," Emma replied.

"Nice comeback."

"Whatever. We should ask Ben, and you know I'm right, so let's go."

As the day was getting late, the twins biked back to the cabin to borrow their parents' rental car. Balky Point was at the north end of the island, about as far away as one could get on the island from Wishing Rock.

"What do you want the car for?" asked their mother.

"Emma wants to see her boyfriend," said Charlie.

"Charlie hopes he can find himself a girlfriend," said Emma.

"Fantastic," said their mother, knowing better than to get involved in such a discussion. "Good luck. Be back for dinner." She handed over the keys, and the twins were out the back door before she could tell them to drive safely.

They wove their way south on the roads, not quite sure how to get there. But, "We're on an island," said Charlie, "How lost can we get?" And he was right; the main road took them straight to the one-building town where they'd spent their winter vacation.

"Home sweet Wishing Rock," said Charlie with a dramatic flair.

As they pulled into the parking lot, they saw several people out at the barbecue area. Emma quickly scanned the group: no Ben. They knew these other people well enough from their visit over Christmas that it would seem rude to walk right past them. And, the fact was, any of them was just as likely to be able to answer their questions as Ben was. It would be weird to walk by, Emma knew, but finding out about the girl was Charlie's mission. Seeing Ben was hers.

Just as Emma shut her car door, though, she saw Ben come out of the building carrying a platter of skewers of meat. With his left foot he held the front door open for his mother, who trailed behind him, a pitcher of lemonade in her left hand and a tray of vegetable skewers precariously balanced on her right. Ben's mother saw the twins first and said something to Ben, who looked in their direction and smiled. He put his tray down on a nearby table and jogged over to meet Emma and Charlie.

"Hey! What brings you back again so soon?" he said, all teeth and smile and charm.

Emma found herself tongue-tied. What was it about this young man that left her speechless and blushing? Why couldn't she have a normal conversation with him like a normal person?

Much to Emma's relief, Charlie stepped in.

"Ben, my man! You still need to tell us more about your trip! We got talking about UFOs and didn't hear about Iceland! How was it?"

"What a country," said Ben. "It's incredible. Ed's mom lives there, so we stayed with her for a few days up in the northwest. We drove around the whole island. Fantastic. Unbelievable. Waterfalls everywhere. You gotta go one day."

"Iceland, that's so cool," said Emma. "Ha! Cool—like, it's cold, get it?" The words slipped out of her mouth even as her brain willed her to stop. *Ix-nay on the umb-day okes-jay,* she said to herself. When she was particularly annoyed with her own stupidity, she often chided herself in Pig Latin. *Don't be such an ork-day.*

Charlie, bless his heart. When it was just the two of them, he could be interminable. But when anyone else was involved, he had her back.

"Cool—cold!" He snorted—literally snorted, relieving the awkward silence. "She's clever," he said in solidarity, nodding his agreement with himself.

Ben laughed too, whether in pity or appreciation Emma didn't know, but it was better than a blank stare. "Actually, it wasn't as cold as I thought it would be, but it did get cold in some places.

The north gets cold especially. You're practically to the Arctic Circle, up there. At night, the sun sets but there's still some light all night long."

Emma slipped off into a reverie, her mind racing back to her honeymoon fantasy, details now filling themselves in. Her, and Ben, and … penguins? Polar bears? … Never mind that. Her, and Ben, and …

"The Land of the Midnight Sun," Ben said, looking at her as though he knew what she was thinking. "That's what they call it."

"The Land of the Midnight Sun." She repeated it like a prayer, a solemn wedding prayer.

Protector or no, Charlie had his limits. He kicked his sister's shin, just a bump, really, covering it up by making it look like he tripped while reaching for a glass of lemonade. But it was enough to get the message across: she needed to stop embarrassing herself, or, worse, him.

"So you came to talk more about Iceland?" said Ben. "Are you thinking about going?"

"No, not Iceland. We're here on business, sir," said Charlie. "Mystery is afoot. Adventure is at hand. Curiosity lies ahead." He stopped to admire his extensive body-part-related comparisons. "Get it? A foot? At hand? A head?"

Ben groaned. "You two are definitely related."

Emma frowned. Gorgeous or not, criticizing her Charlie was not fair game. She reached her arms around her brother in a protective side hug, though it was as much to give her comfort as anything. Emma was always uneasy in groups and many social situations. Charlie could charm a crowd and have them wrapped around his little finger in ten seconds flat. Emma, on the other hand, never knew what to say. As a result, Charlie often went out while Emma stayed home. She said it didn't bother her, but deep down, it did.

"We have a very interesting question," she said. "Have you been up to the lighthouse at Balky Point? That's not the interesting question. That's the question leading to the interesting question," she rambled. "There's another question after that. That's the interesting one."

Charlie squeezed her to make her stop.

Ben, of course, had been to Balky Point. "That's where all the kids on the island go to make out, or get lost, or just think," he said. "Why?"

"Have you ever looked at the pictures on the walls?" asked Charlie.

"That's the interesting question," said Emma, half to herself.

A red tinge rose up Ben's neck. "We don't—I don't usually go inside when I go there," he admitted. "A lot more sitting on the cliffs and ... looking out at the sea. And stuff."

"You should look around inside more," Emma said, annoyed at the implication. The honeymoon vision floating in a bubble over her head disappeared, popped by a young woman as blonde as the girl in the pictures.

"What's inside?" asked Ben.

Charlie explained. "Photos on the walls, going back a century."

Ben shrugged: this was exciting, how, exactly?

"But," Charlie continued, "the same girl is in all of them."

Ben furrowed his eyebrows in exaggerated confusion. "The same girl? You mean in a few pictures?"

"A lot of pictures. Decades apart," said Charlie. He held out his phone for Ben to see, the same picture he'd shown Ben the other night. "This girl."

This time, Ben's confusion was real. "There are old pictures of the girl from the parade in the lighthouse?"

"Interesting, isn't it?" said Emma, feeling vindicated. "Same girl. She's in more than half the pictures. Her, and another guy, an older guy. Not recent pictures. Old pictures. More than a century old."

"How is that possible?" said Charlie, affecting a deep movie an-
nouncer voice. "Explain that, compadre. First UFOs, then this.
Dogwinkle Island, you are a crazy place. In a world where dogs and
cats marry and fish walk on land, where giraffes can swim, where
north is east and time travels backward ..." He trailed off. "Yeah,
that's all I got," he said, his voice back to normal.

Ben shook his head. "I don't have a clue who she is. Never saw her
before you showed me that picture."

Charlie was deflated, Emma disappointed. "But Obi-Ben-Kenobi,
you were our only hope," said Charlie. "How will we find her now?"

Ben thought a minute, his gaze wandering to his friends at the
barbecue, skewers smoking on the grill, people laughing and chatting. His eyes lit up, and he snapped his fingers. "A potluck!" he
said. "Potlucks bring out people. We'll have an island-wide potluck.
Mom'll organize it, no problem. Her sister is coming into town
tomorrow. I'm sure they were going to do something anyway. We'll
just invite everyone. Maybe we can bring that girl out of hiding."

"What if they're gone from the island already?" said Emma. "We
don't want to miss them."

"You said they've been in pictures on the walls for decades," said
Ben. "Seems they're here to stay."

Emma had to admit Ben had a point. "But a potluck?" she said.
"Doesn't that take time to plan?"

"Are you kidding?" said Ben. "In Wishing Rock, we potluck like
we breathe."

chapter two

In the end, there was slightly more to putting together a potluck than Ben had indicated, but not much. Ben's mother and aunt, well-versed in potlucks, worked their magic, with Emma helping as much as she was able. By the next weekend, everything was in place for a potluck, hoedown, and, at Ed's insistence, a karaoke stage. Despite having just come down off the parade events less than a week before, or maybe because of it, everyone was in a party mood. Come Saturday afternoon, nearly every person on the island was in attendance.

"Small island," Ed had explained. "We gotta make our own fun."

Emma had agreed to help with the refreshment table; Charlie had finagled himself a job as D.J. The karaoke stage would only operate between hoedown sessions (all had agreed that no one needed nonstop karaoke), and Charlie was quite pleased with himself for managing to get out of doing much work.

Emma, on the other hand, was an emotional wreck. In deciding what to wear, she had tried to reach the perfect balance between actual casual and glamorous casual—that is, casual that looked casual but actually required hours of work to achieve. She'd meticulously applied her makeup but then sneezed moments after swiping mascara on her lashes, thus smearing it all around her eyes. This necessitated her washing her whole face and starting over. *Stupid allergies,* she grumbled mentally. While brushing her teeth, she dropped a clump of toothpaste on her carefully chosen shirt. The toothpaste came out with water but left a stiff and shiny spot on the fabric. Frantically ironing her back-up outfit, Emma wondered what else could possibly go wrong. If she wanted to impress Ben, tonight was her best chance. She sat in her room for a while, practicing the art of conversation to try to build her confidence, but in her mind she never could get much beyond, "Hi, Ben!" What to say next? *No wonder I never get any dates,* she thought.

Even as he mocked Emma's struggles, Charlie himself was putting extra effort into his appearance for the evening. Rather than just swishing a hand through his wavy light-auburn hair, Charlie ran a brush through it, and he checked his dark blue shirt for stains before putting it on with his khaki shorts. Thus finished with his own preparations, he went to Emma's room to check on hers. Seeing her sitting on the end of her bed talking to herself, he punched her on the shoulder.

"Dork," he said.

She punched him back. "Dork," she said.

On arriving at Wishing Rock shortly before noon, the twins were met by the conversation and activity that regularly hummed through the tiny town. Emma rushed off to the refreshment table to keep her mind occupied; Charlie immediately and easily mingled with the locals and introduced himself to people he didn't already know, his eyes always on the lookout for The Girl.

Soon enough, the party was going strong, and both Emma and Charlie forgot their missions. Rather, Charlie forgot his; Emma was struggling with hers. Ben's aunt was busy calling the hoedown steps, and people from all over the island were swinging and stepping and laughing. Emma slowly maneuvered herself closer to Ben, trying not to be obvious about her intentions while at the same time trying to get his attention, smile at him, ignore him, and pretend to be nonchalant yet attractive. She tried to join in the dancing, but the concentration required to follow the hoedown calls while at the same time flirting without looking like she was flirting exhausted her introverted soul.

So when The Girl appeared, Emma didn't even notice until she felt Charlie's elbow poke most unceremoniously into her side.

"That's her!" he whispered loudly.

"What?" Emma said, barely able to hear him over the music and the general party pandemonium.

Charlie rolled his eyes in a giant circle to point in the direction of the drinks table, and nodded his head with little subtlety. "The Girl!" he said. "She's here!"

Emma looked in the direction Charlie indicated and saw The Girl standing there. An older man stood next to her, though it wasn't clear whether they were together or simply standing next to each other. They spoke a few words, then The Girl nodded and the man walked away. It was definitely The Girl from the pictures, Emma thought. She'd stared at the photos on the wall of the lighthouse and on Charlie's phone enough that of this, she was certain. She exchanged an excited glance with Charlie, who was grinning from ear to ear. Their plan to draw out this girl from wherever she was hiding had worked! Emma had had her doubts as to whether a potluck was interesting enough to bring in a stranger, but she was not going to put down Ben or his suggestion. And somehow, magically, it worked!

Ben, who had not been completely oblivious to nor opposed to Emma's flirtations, noticed that Emma and Charlie had stopped two-stepping and were now looking off to the side. He came and joined them, giving Emma a quick side-hug.

"Hey, guys! What are we looking at?" he said. Then, seeing The Girl, his eyes lit up. "That's her!"

Suddenly, Emma was not so sure about this plan anymore. Although she had been the one to bring Ben in on this mystery from the start, she now wished she hadn't. Looking at The Girl, she knew she couldn't compete. Where her own shoulder-length hair was a nice-enough dark auburn, The Girl's was shimmery blonde, almost white, the color of starlight, glowing in the late afternoon sun. Her skin was flawless, as if it were lit from within. She moved with grace and poise. Emma was certain The Girl was also confident and smart, outgoing and funny and fun. All the things she knew her own awkward, slightly weird, strange humored, self-conscious, shy self not to be.

And, of course, both Ben and Charlie were gawking at The Girl.

"Well, well, well, my man!" said Charlie. "No time like the present!" Regardless of whether he saw Ben as competition, he was not going to wait for the other young man to make the first move. Before either Ben or Emma could say a word, Charlie was across the dance floor and by The Girl's side.

By the time Ben and Emma caught up, Charlie already had The Girl laughing.

Manifesting the warm, welcoming confidence that Emma remembered so well, Ben joined in the laughter without knowing what was funny and immediately extended his hand. "I'm Ben," he said, holding The Girl's hand slightly longer than Emma thought was really necessary.

The Girl flashed a smile of perfect teeth. "I'm Eve," she said. "Nice to meet you."

"Nice to meet you, too! I live here," said Ben, his arms wide to indicate all of Wishing Rock, "and I thought I knew just about everyone, but I don't think we've met. Do you live on the island?"

The charisma and self-assurance emanating from both Ben and Eve made Emma wince with envy. She couldn't begrudge Ben being nice to The Girl. After all, she liked that about him: he was kind and friendly to everyone. Still, she felt a lump of jealousy growing in her chest, and part of her wanted to run away. Emma could sense that Charlie now shared her own misgivings about this plan. This was not going according to script at all.

"No," said Eve, averting her eyes, "we're just visiting."

"From Seattle?" said Charlie, reasserting his presence. Reaching for an empty cup with one hand, he held out an open palm to the punch bowl while looking at Eve, his raised eyebrows asking whether she'd like a drink. She shook her head. Charlie dipped the long-handled scoop into the punch bowl and poured himself a glass, then poured another for his sister.

"No, we're not local." Eve smiled and offered no more information. "Are you two from Wishing Rock, as well?" She looked from Charlie to Emma.

"We're just visiting the island for the summer," said Emma, sipping her drink carefully so as not to spill it. "We're staying in a cabin up north a bit. You said 'we'—who's 'we'? Is it that man you were with a couple minutes ago?"

Eve nodded. "That's my dad," she said.

"So, where are you from?" Charlie asked. "'Not local' doesn't tell us much! Unless 'Not Local' is the name of a city I haven't heard of?" He laughed at his own joke.

Eve laughed, too, a soft, gentle laugh that Emma suspected would be described as "like the wind." "No, we're not from around here. A ways away. Nowhere you've heard of, I'm sure."

"But you've been to the island before?" asked Emma. Normally, she wouldn't be so direct, but this girl was clearly evading their questions.

And she managed to do so again, as her father walked up and draped an arm over his daughter's shoulders. "Hello!" he said. "I'm Milo." He reached out a hand to Charlie.

"Charlie," said Charlie, shaking Milo's hand.

"Ben," said Ben, next in line for the handshakes.

"I'm Emma," said Emma, "Charlie's twin. Nice to meet you. We were just asking Emma about your past visits to the island?"

Like father, like daughter. He avoided the question and instead turned to Eve. "We have to go now," he said; then, to Charlie, Ben, and Emma, "I'm so sorry ... uh, some friends just called. They need us to ..." He trailed off without finishing.

Eve looked torn but resigned. "Nice to meet you all," she said. "Maybe we'll meet again one day."

"I hope so," said Charlie, setting his emptied cup on the table, "we're only here for a couple more weeks. Come find us if you can. We'd love to see you."

Eve smiled and nodded. Without another word, she and her father left.

"That's just bunk," Ben said, once the father and daughter were out of hearing distance. "What friends are they talking about? Everyone's here." He looked around at the hoedown crowd. While clearly not everyone on the island was actually in attendance, there were indeed many people on the dance floor and at the tables, chatting and catching up and having a grand old time.

Emma agreed. "Total bunk," she said. Regardless, she was relieved to see Eve go. But what had the other young woman meant with her cryptic, "Maybe we'll meet again one day"? From the pictures at the lighthouse, it was obvious she had been around for some time. Yet for some reason Ben had never met her, and she seemed to think it was possible they'd never meet again. They'd completed their mission: to find this strange girl. But meeting her left them with more questions than answers.

The hoedown was over, but a few stragglers had gathered out on the lawn, dissecting the day, discussing who had shown up and who hadn't, who had said what, who had danced with whom. The clean-up committee had more or less finished their tasks, leaving those who stayed behind to clean up after themselves before going in for the night. The group, including Emma, Charlie, and Ben, was sitting in a circle in the encroaching dark, some bundled in blankets, watching the sky as the stars started to come out, giving their presence to the night. Only the lights from the building illuminated the evening.

Wishing Rock was made up of a menagerie of residents, some of whom had lived there for decades. None of them had recognized the strangers. And so Ben explained the unsolved mystery, with the help of Charlie and Emma—how Eve was in all the pictures at the Balky Point lighthouse, how she'd been at the parade, how they still knew nothing about her.

"We were just curious about her," said Ben. "Something seems strange in Eveland. Still does. Now more than ever."

"That's why we had this potluck," added Charlie. "We wanted to find her."

"Well, I'd say you accomplished that," said Ed, who was bundled up with his wife, Ruby, tightly wound together in their hand-tied quilt like two caterpillars in a cocoon.

"Yeah, but not really. Like she said, who knows if we'll ever see her again?" said Charlie, feeling alone in his own blanket, wishing a young blonde companion would join him.

"I'll bet you a million dollars you'll see her again," said Ed with a mischievous grin.

At this, Ben, who knew Ed's sense of humor and also knew he

wasn't much of a gambler, was suspicious. He narrowed his eyes in the dim light. "Why? What do you know?"

Ed replied by looking behind Ben and pointing with his chin to the space beyond the young man. "Too bad for me you didn't take that bet. I'd have held you to it, you know." He winked.

Ben, Charlie, and Emma twirled around. In the fading light they could just see two figures approaching from the parking lot. The secretive father and daughter had returned and were walking toward the gathered group.

The boys and Emma got up to greet the pair, meeting them a bit away from the rest of the group. *Something's different,* thought Emma. Hadn't Eve's hair—now silvery in the moonlight—been loose before? It was in a ponytail now. *But that's not too unusual,* she thought; *girls put their hair up and down all the time. As often as they changed ...*

"Your clothes," she said, out loud. "You changed."

Emma was sure she saw a fleeting moment of panic on Eve's face, but perhaps it was just a trick of the moonlight.

But then: "*You* changed too," Emma said to Milo. "You both changed your clothes."

Piquing Emma's suspicions, Milo and Eve ignored her completely.

"Hey, again, kids! Say, we forgot to ask you something when we were here," Milo said with an affectation of nonchalance. He presented a picture he was holding. "Have you seen this man? Ever? Not just recently, but ... ever?"

Something about the way he said the words made Emma pause. "Ever? Does he live here? For how long?"

Charlie pulled out his phone and turned on the flashlight to look at the picture. The bright light seemed harsh in the soft early evening, casting eerie shadows, blotting out stars, and making the night seem far darker than it was. The photo showed a young man, maybe early twenties, with harsh, uninviting eyes, the color of a raven. He was neither frowning nor smiling. The man's ebony hair, shorter at the neck but longer on top, covered his forehead and curled slightly into his eyes. He was dressed all in black, dark like the night sky.

Milo smiled at Emma's question, but the light of the flashlight made the shadows of his cheeks creep up over his eyes. "That's sort of hard to say. Just … have you seen him?"

Charlie, too, was growing somewhat wary. "Do you have pictures from when he was younger? I mean, if he's been here a while."

Eve cleared her throat. "Well, you see, he would always look like this, even if you saw him years ago." She shifted her weight from one leg to the other.

"Just like you?" said Charlie. "Like you haven't changed in a hundred years? I saw you at the parade and thought you were cute. But then Emma saw you in all the pictures at the lighthouse, and …"

"… we knew we had to find you," finished Ben.

Eve looked at the tall, dark-haired young man. "You were looking for me?" She laughed. In the light, it was hard to tell whether she blushed. She shook her head, dismissing the idea. "No, we just need to find this man. His name is Vik."

Emma, frustrated by jealousy, stomped her foot like a two-year-old. "No," she said. "No, you can't get off that easily. You've been avoiding our questions all night. Who are you, how are you possibly in all those pictures, looking the same every time, years apart, decades apart? Who is Vik? Why wouldn't he have aged either? What is going on? This Vik, if you think he's here, why don't you just find his house? Where does he live? Who are you?" She stopped and breathed heavily, as though winded by the weight of all her swirling thoughts.

Eve turned her head to Milo, a question in her eyes. He nodded.

"Well. That's just the thing, isn't it." Eve glanced back at the rest of the group on the lawn, chatting amongst themselves with great animation, all but oblivious to the conversation going on in the shadows.

"Can you keep a secret?" she said.

chapter three

"All right, so, the thing is ... we're aliens," Eve blurted out, the words she'd been holding in erupting out of her like a burst dam.

Eve, her father, the twins, and Ben had found an empty setting of hay bales farther away from the sharp ears of Wishing Rock residents. After settling down and a bit of hemming and hawing, Eve delivered the implausible news.

Emma, Ben, and Charlie stared, saying nothing at first. What was there to say? *Of course, aliens,* Emma thought. *Why wouldn't they be aliens? And if they were, of course they'd just tell everyone. That makes perfect sense.* She couldn't even think of how to respond to such an outrageous story.

Charlie spoke first. "So, you mean, alien, like from a foreign country? Are you ... Canadian? Eh?" He chuckled.

Ben, who had magically landed a spot on the two-seater hay bale with Eve, laughed, but then nodded. He nudged Eve with his elbow. "So, Canadian? Canada's cool. I like maple syrup."

"No," said Milo, from his own hay bale next to his daughter. "Not Canadian. Alien aliens. We're ... not from this planet."

Eve nudged Ben back. "Technically, from our point of view, you guys are the aliens," she said, punctuating her statement with her twinkling ethereal laugh.

"*We* are the aliens," repeated Emma. She was sitting on the hay bale on Ben's other side, but not the same hay bale as Ben. A hay bale from a distant planet, as far as she was concerned. An alien hay bale. An invisible alien hay bale. "But you're on *our* planet." This made no sense.

"Well, yes," said Eve. "But we're layered on your planet, or you're layered on ours. We're layered. So in a way none of us is an alien. Or all of us are."

This is definitely making less and less sense, thought Emma. *Who are these people, and what are they playing at?* "'Layered'? What do you mean by 'layered'?" She looked around. As far as she—or any rational person—could see, there was one planet here, and one planet only.

"Where to start," said Eve. She looked at her father for help.

"Okay," began Milo. He leaned forward, elbows on knees, hands gesticulating to help him explain. "First thing to know is that this island is what's known as a 'thin spot.'"

Charlie shook his head. "Wait, I'm still getting past the part where you're not Canadian. You're *alien* aliens? Like, you're from another planet? Is that possible? That's not possible. Travel through space and all that, I thought it would take millions of years for any aliens to get here, and that's if they even exist." He looked at Eve. "You are definitely not millions of years old," he said. He looked at Milo. "I doubt you are, either."

Milo laughed. "Thank you, Charlie, I am indeed not millions of years old, and neither is Eve. I suppose we misspoke. We're not from another planet. Rather, we're not *just* from another planet. We're from another universe."

Ben stood up, this new bit of information too much to take sitting down. "Another universe? Are you kidding us? Not just another planet but another universe? Do you understand Latin roots?

The 'uni' in 'universe,' do you know what that means? That means 'one.' Because there's one universe. Like the word 'unique,' it doesn't mean there's more than one like it, it means there's just the one. Just the one … que. Whatever a que is. But there's just one of it. There's one universe, and this is it." He squinted at Milo. "Who are you, really? What do you want?" He paced as he talked, and Charlie took the opportunity to slip from his own solitary hay bale into the coveted spot Ben had left open next to Eve.

"*I* believe you," Charlie said. "I mean, I'm keeping an open mind. I had no idea aliens would be so pretty. This is why I believe in the school of life, people." He winked at his sister. "You don't learn things like this in high school."

With a grin, Eve reached out and gave Charlie a one-arm hug. "Silly Earthlings," she joked. "No, we're real aliens, Ben. No lies. Total truth. And we're really from another universe. That's what Dad was about to explain."

Ben sat back down, this time taking the open spot next to Emma. Emma subtly shifted herself ever so slightly closer to the warmth of the young man's riled-up body. "If you're aliens, what are you doing on *this* island?" she said. Then, realizing her insult to Ben's home, added, "Not that there's anything wrong with Dogwinkle. It's a beautiful place."

Ben absentmindedly patted Emma's knee. Emma's heart fluttered in her throat.

"As I was saying," said Milo, "Dogwinkle is a thin spot. Think of a quilt. You know those simple quilts some people make, just layer upon layer of cotton batting, tied together every few inches with pieces of yarn? Imagine that each layer of cotton batting is a universe. And those points where everything is tied together, those are thin spots. At thin spots, the universes are right on top of each other, almost intermingling. At thin spots, everything is possible."

Over at the other group of party-goers, Emma saw her parents, Ed and his wife, Ben's parents, all the others. They were laughing, raising their glasses of wine or punch now and then to emphasize a point of conversation (those who were not completely bundled up in blankets, anyway), oblivious to the idea that there could be— Emma was only willing to give the idea a "*could* be" status—people from another universe just yards away from them. She wanted to stay annoyed with Eve, but Emma couldn't help but be intrigued. Another universe? Layered right on top of her own? If—*if*—that were possible, if it were true, suddenly Earth felt both tiny and infinite.

Emma decided to go along with this alien deceit, for the time being, for fun. "So Dogwinkle is a thin spot. What difference does that make? Why did you pick this island? Why are you here? And that guy, Vik, why is he here? Why are you looking for him? Is he an alien, too? Is he on the run from the law? Are you bounty hunters? And how long have you been here? We saw pictures of you at the lighthouse. You've been here for more than a hundred years. Can you please explain?" Emma felt as though she had a universe of questions growing inside her.

"Whoa, whoa, whoa!" said Milo. "One thing at a time! We're here because it's a thin spot. On our planet we've only discovered interuniverse travel, travel between the universes, in the last hundred years—about a hundred of your years, that is. Our scientists are working on new discoveries every day, but at this point, we only know how to travel at thin spots. That's where we've found the elevators."

"*Elevators?*" gasped Charlie in disbelief. This was only getting better. First aliens, now aliens traveling in elevators. "You came here in an *elevator?*"

Milo held up his hands. "No! Ha, sorry, my mistake. We just

call them elevators. They're not literal elevators. They're … doorways, I suppose. Portals. Here on Earth, as far as we've discovered, every elevator is in a lighthouse. That's rare in the universes, actually, and it indicates that maybe someone knew about the elevators, somehow, when the lighthouses were being built. Most elevators on other planets are just in random spots. The middle of a field, at the edge of an island, could be anywhere. But here, they're all in lighthouses."

"Lighthouses are elevators to other universes?" Charlie's voice was a mixture of incredulity and delight. He couldn't wait to hear what was coming next.

"Venn diagrams," said Ben. "He said the elevators are in lighthouses, not that all lighthouses are elevators. Elevators in lighthouses are a subset of lighthouses, not the other way around." He looked at Milo for confirmation.

"Exactly right, Ben," said Milo. Ben beamed. "All elevators seem to be in lighthouses on Earth, but not all lighthouses on Earth have elevators. We haven't investigated every lighthouse yet, of course, nor found every elevator. We've been busy."

Emma nodded a small nod. "Vik," she said. As though somehow, that made everything make sense.

"Yes, Vik," said Milo. "We need to find him before he destroys everything."

"Wait," said Charlie. "This is all … you're going too fast. So to recap, you are aliens from another planet in another universe, and you traveled here in an elevator to catch a bad guy. But tell me this: you've been here for decades without getting any older. How do you explain that?"

Eve joined her father's narrative. "We know—or we're pretty sure—Vik is either on Earth, or at the very least he's somewhere that's accessed by the Dogwinkle elevator. Could be in another universe. We don't know. But this is where the energy trails lead, so this is where we're looking."

"The Balky Point lighthouse," said Ben. "That's your elevator? That's how you get to your planet, your universe?"

Eve nodded, as though this were the easiest thing in the world—in the universes—to understand.

"All those times my brother went up to that lighthouse to make out with girls, and he never knew," mumbled Ben. "Elevator to another planet. Now *that* would have been a date!"

Emma squirmed.

"So why do you want to catch this Vik?" asked Charlie. "What's he done that warrants a cross-universe quest?"

"As I said, we've only known about this interuniverse travel ability for a hundred of your years or so," said Milo. "The spots have been there forever, we assume. We have scientists studying the thin spots, but our knowledge is just in its infancy. Who knows what we'll discover? Before we learned about this, we knew as little about aliens as you all do. Or did. We knew aliens could exist; we knew that, statistically, they probably did. We knew it was possible there were more universes than just our own, but we'd never traveled to find alien life. Never imagined we would, or at least, I never imagined I would."

Emma saw Eve glance quickly at her father, her eyes filled with sadness and something else, but she couldn't read any more into the look. She tried to imagine herself as an alien. Everything that seemed so real to her, everything that seemed so normal and usual and comforting to her, to someone else, somewhere else, was alien. To Eve, she was alien.

Then she realized something. "Hold on a minute. You look just like us. Do all aliens look like humans? And also—you were wearing different clothes when you were here earlier tonight. Just a couple hours ago. Is it still today for you? Did you travel in time, too?"

Charlie looked disappointed that this idea hadn't even occurred to him, but he was right on top of the concept. "Time travel! Do you travel through time? Is that how you look the same in all the pictures? That's it! You're time-traveling aliens! Oh my gosh. This is crack. This is insane. Time-traveling aliens." He gazed at the beautiful girl sitting next to him, returning her earlier one-arm hug with a side hug of his own. "Eve, my favorite time-traveling alien." Then, he paused. "Um, are you … a … girl?" He unwound his arm from the alien beside him.

Emma cut in, not really wanting to hear the answer. "So. Okay. Let's say you are, in fact, real aliens."

"We are," said Eve, lifting her chin.

"Why are you here, then? What made you come to Earth?" Emma asked.

Charlie's discomfort left him. "Yes! Are you planning an invasion? Do we have twenty-four hours to live? Are the spaceships coming to attack us?" He looked up to the sky for signs of imminent danger.

Emma sighed. Leave it to Charlie to be so excited at the prospect of the End of the World. Sure, it was exciting in theory, but in reality, she guessed probably not so much.

Eve also chose to ignore Charlie's digression. "We told you about Vik," she said.

"Yes," said Emma, "but who is he? Why do you want to find him? Why did *he* come here, and why is it a problem?"

Milo shrugged. "It's been interesting coming here. This is our first trip, you see, mine and Eve's. And even though we've been on Earth for a hundred of your years, in our time it's just been a few months. A year, maybe. Time is difficult to ascertain sometimes. All we can say, really," he looked at Eve, warning her not to say more, "is that Vik is trying to make trouble."

"Trouble?" Charlie asked.

Milo either didn't hear Charlie or didn't answer. "We think he's been traveling through time, too," he said. "We think some of the natural disasters you've had here through the years haven't been so natural. You know that big earthquake of 2006?"

"It was a 6.8," Ben told Charlie and Emma, "lasted almost a minute. I remember that. I was up on top of the building, hunched under a big desk, and I thought Wishing Rock was done for. Thought for sure it was my day to die. Balky Point was right at the epicenter—wait. Was that related to Vik? To why you're here?"

"We think maybe it was. We think some of the unusual things that have been happening on your Earth have actually been because of Vik. No one's noticed, because your global warming and climate change and general humanity are wreaking havoc of their own. But a few things, we think, have been Vik," said Milo.

"That's crazy," said Ben. "For how long? How long has Vik been bringing the crazy? And why?"

"At least a hundred years," said Eve, "Maybe more. We first landed here in your year 1874, and we've been moving forward a few years at a time, looking for signs that he's been around."

"We're sort of going on instinct as much as science," said Milo with a sigh. "Or more. Hoping that if we see a clue, we'll recognize it as a clue."

Charlie was less interested in Vik, however, than in the idea of traveling the universe—the universes. "How many elevators did you say there are?" Emma could see it in his eyes: escape. Adventure. Trouble of his own kind.

"In total?" said Milo. "Millions. Billions. Finite, but for all intents and purposes, uncountable. And we don't know whether more are being created. If it's a natural occurrence, then as the universes expand, new elevators are probably created all the time. If not, who knows. There could be a society in some far off world where all they do all day long is build new elevators. And since time is a tricky substance, who knows if they're doing it now, in the past, or in the future."

Charlie shook his head rapidly like a confused cartoon character. "Doing it in the future? Right. Totally a normal statement. Okay, so how many elevators are there on Earth, then? Round numbers."

"Not as many," said Milo. "We don't know for sure, obviously—we've been busy chasing down Vik. But our scientists estimate it at around a dozen, maybe two dozen at most. They're not everywhere. Just enough to get by."

"Two dozen!" said Emma. "Why Dogwinkle, then? What's so special about this island that it merits an elevator?" The idea that there were only a few handfuls more of these thin spots on her planet was mind-boggling. Actually, the idea that they existed at all was mind-boggling. But for one to be right here, at their randomly chosen vacation spot, that was unbelievable.

"We don't know," said Milo, his hesitation suggesting once again that he knew more than he would say. "It's isolated, but everything would have been isolated when the elevators first appeared. Islands seem to be popular spots. Like we said, all the elevators on Earth are at lighthouses. Coincidence? We don't know."

"So, no offense, Milo, but what good are you if you don't really know anything?" said Charlie.

Milo laughed. "One of the great traits shared by you Earthlings and people on our planet is curiosity. We don't know, but we're learning. We have scientists working on it. We're not far ahead of you in terms of these discoveries. We have a long way to go yet."

Ben shook his head. "You keep talking about your scientists. But where are they? All of space and time, where are you hiding them?"

Eve looked at her watch to check the time—about nine o'clock—then at her father for permission, which he granted with a nod. "Do you want to meet them?" she asked.

"YES!" cried the three Earthlings in unison.

"To the lighthouse," said Milo with a flourish.

chapter four

Bumping along the winding dirt road from Wishing Rock to Balky Point in the bed of Milo's rusty blue truck, Charlie and Ben in the back with her and Milo and Eve in the cab, Emma's mind flooded with questions. Even the mundane was suspect: how did Milo get a driver's license? Surely he didn't have a birth certificate or proof of any sort of Earthly residency. Or did he? Maybe the scientists they were heading to see were masters at the art of forgery as well? Or magic? Or deception? Maybe they could influence humans' minds: a simple "This is not the fake driver's license you're looking for" and the DMV worker would look away, unaware of the alien spell, not fully sure what was happening and certain to forget everything the moment the aliens were gone? And further, was Milo a safe driver? The speed at which he took some of the narrow curves suggested otherwise. Did they have cars on their planet? Where, again, exactly, was their planet? Did they even say? Layered, she remembered. What did that mean? Was this all a hoax? Island chicanery? Emma struggled to smooth her hair as it blew wildly in the wind and started looking around the truck for hidden cameras.

"Do you think Milo has a driver's license?" said Ben to Emma, his voice raised over the rumble of the wheels hitting rocks and the howl of the wind. He and Emma were riding in the truck bed facing backward; Charlie was sitting on the side, turned front, face up, eyes closed, smile wide as he soaked in the moonlight and the adventure.

Emma blinked with surprise. Had she voiced her thoughts out loud? Was she speaking when she thought she was thinking?

"I was just wondering the same thing," she said. She couldn't help but smile. Ben laughed, and Emma's smile grew.

"Crazy," he said. "Can you believe this? I have no idea what I'm even expecting when we get there. They seem like nice people, but this whole thing is ridiculous. Aliens!" He shook his head. "Did not see that one coming."

Emma rubbed her arms and zipped her jacket up to her chin. The chill of the night and the rush of air as they flew down the road were making her cold. "I know," she said. "Part of me wants to believe it, but there's no way it's true. Seriously. Still, I'm curious what they're up to."

"I've always been curious about space," said Ben, looking up at the narrow path of sky visible above the tree-lined road. "It would be cool if it were true."

Emma nodded just as the force from swerving around a tight curve tossed her halfway into Ben's lap. She took her time in dragging herself up and away from Ben. If, in fact, this was all a joke, she thought, it was not without its benefits. She was pleased that the shiny intergalactic girl was inside the cab, and she had Ben to herself.

"Me too," she said. "I like science. I've sometimes thought I might do something science-y for a career, even, but I don't know what."

Ben turned abruptly to face Emma. "Really? Me too. Actually, I don't know. My brother has always known what he wanted to do—he's studying to be a doctor now—but I've never known. I mean, like, he knew when he was a kid. That young. I've never had a clue. Everyone focuses on my brother, anyway, so there's not as much pressure on me, but it would be nice to have some idea what I want to do." He paused. "Maybe science." He looked at the stars. "Maybe space."

"Maybe space," she repeated. Truth was, she had no idea either. But suddenly space sounded really, really appealing.

Emma grabbed a tighter hold of the side of the truck and adjusted her gaze carefully so her face was looking forward, but she could see Ben out of the corner of her eye. It was dark, but her eyes had adjusted to the night, and the moon was almost full. Ben's long legs stretched out next to hers into the middle of the truck bed. She thought maybe he'd gotten taller since December, but sitting next to him she couldn't tell. Her eyes were drawn to his hands, which looked both soft and strong at the same time. Gentle but confident hands, she thought. Could hands be confident?

A yell from inside the cab startled her back to the present. Before she could figure out what Milo had bellowed, the truck jerked up and down as Milo drove with reckless abandon through a deep pothole.

"Ah bit mah tung," said Charlie as he righted himself from the unexpected topple.

Milo yelled back out the driver's window, "Sorry about that!"

But Emma was not upset. She had landed in Ben's lap again, and he was helping her get back up. Definitely gentle hands, she thought.

Milo slowed down a bit after that, and it wasn't too long before he eased the truck to a stop at the lighthouse parking lot. Charlie was already halfway out of the vehicle before Milo turned off the engine. He rubbed his hands with glee.

"Aliens in Dogwinkle!" he said. "Aliens in Dogwinkle! In Dogwinkle! Em, imagine if we'd convinced Mom and Dad to take us to Hawaii? What would we have? A beach, margaritas, hot women in bikinis, sand, surf, … but NO ALIENS. Em. Do you hear what I'm saying? NO ALIENS."

"You can't drink yet," she replied, climbing out of the truck bed with help from Ben, but what she thought was, *And no Ben.*

"So, where's the elevator?" Charlie asked, as Eve and Milo slammed the stubborn truck doors behind them. He strained his neck, peering around the base of the building. "We didn't see an elevator when we were here before."

"Like I said, it's not an actual elevator," said Milo, laughing at Charlie's exuberance. "Just a closet, really."

"A portal," said Eve. "A doorway. Not an elevator."

"First floor, houseware. Second floor, men's clothes. Third floor, ALIENS," Charlie said. Under his breath, he added, "Aliens aliens aliens aliens aliens aliens!"

"Calm down there, cowboy," said Ben, with a glance at Eve.

Milo switched on a light as they walked through the unlocked front door and into the lobby where Emma and Charlie had seen all the pictures of Eve. Shadows crept across the floor, and a shiver crawled up Emma's spine. *Is this why people think the place is haunted?* she wondered. *Is it really aliens?*

Ben headed straight to the wall of photos and scrutinized them closely. When he found Eve in the first picture, a gentle smile of familiarity spread over his face. He pointed at the image. "It *is* you," he said with delight.

"You … you … you." His discoveries traced the same path Emma and Charlie had taken before. "You." He pointed at each picture in progression as he found Eve's bright blonde hair and intense eyes amongst the crowds. "You've been here since before I was born. Where have you been all my life?" He caught her eye and smiled.

Charlie coughed loudly, a cough that sounded suspiciously like a word.

"What was that?" said Ben.

"Just the dust," said Charlie, waving imaginary particles from his shoulders and the air in front of his face.

Oblivious to the drama, Eve had made her way to a closet marked "Storage: Staff Only." She stood by it expectantly, looking at the others, waiting.

Emma noticed Eve's attention to the door. "The storage closet?" she said. "The elevator is in a storage closet?"

"Life is full of mystery," said Eve, as she opened the closet door.

"Wait, that door was locked before," said Charlie. "I tried all the doors. That was locked."

"You tried all the doors?" said Emma. "When did you try all the doors? Why did you try all the doors? You hoodlum."

"Why *wouldn't* I try all the doors?" Charlie said incredulously.

"You wouldn't have been able to get in. It was locked," said Eve. "Let's just say I have a master key."

With the door opened, the interior of the room was revealed. Emma didn't realize she'd been excited until she felt the cool rush of disappointment spread over her. Barely enough for a storage closet, the room was just a few feet deep and maybe six feet wide. And completely, utterly, vacant.

"The universe is smaller than I thought," deadpanned Charlie, peering around the doorway into the meager space within.

"Not much storage in here," said Emma.

"It's not actually a storage room," said Eve.

Obviously, thought Emma. "Do the lighthouse staff know?" she asked. "You'd think eventually they'd get suspicious."

"The staff know," said Milo, herding the teenagers into the room and filing in behind them. "They're spot keepers. They work with us."

"Aliens aliens aliens aliens aliens aliens," chanted Charlie quietly as he shuffled forward into the closet, his eyes sparkling.

"But it's just a room," said Emma, studying the cramped space to see if she was missing something. "There's no universe in here." She exchanged a glance with Ben: *Are they serious?* Again she wondered if Eve and Milo were frauds … frauds, that was, who had now lured three unsuspecting minors (well, Ben was of age, but that wasn't the point) into a closet. A closet! What had they been thinking! She started to panic. Did she have her Swiss army knife with her, the one her Dad had given her for her last birthday? Of course not. Of course she didn't. Why would she carry it with her? No reason to expect she was going to be abducted. Abducted by fake aliens! The poetic license of it made her laugh out loud.

"Shut the door," said Eve to her father—or was it really her father, Emma wondered? He obliged after switching on a light.

Emma looked to see whether she could escape. Milo was blocking the door. *Clever, isn't it,* she thought, *how he casually placed himself right in the path to freedom.* Emma mentally scanned her body for assets. Why oh why had she cut her fingernails just two days prior? They could have been good weapons. Knees and elbows, she decided. It would have to be knees and elbows. She started to position herself to knee Milo right in the groin when—

"Eve, open the Hub."

Emma sighed with relief, expecting the door behind Milo to open again. But instead, the entire back wall of the closet separated, two panels pulling apart from the center of a wall that just moments before had seemed to be a seamless wall.

A warm natural light filled the closet. Emma gasped. Charlie cried out, "What the …!" then started his chant again. "Aliens aliens aliens …"

"Welcome to the Hub," said Milo, grinning.

As the doors parted in front of Eve, a giant room came into sight. More than a room. *A whole other world?* wondered Emma. She had walked around the lighthouse before, and she knew for certain this space did not fit inside the other side of the closet; did not, for that matter, fit inside the entire lighthouse. Not by a long shot. She decided this was not a fake alien abduction after all … and she hoped it wasn't a real one, either. Alternatively, she hoped she had not gone completely insane.

"What … what is this?" said Ben, trying to take in everything he was seeing. "Is this your planet?"

"Bigger on the inside," said Emma quietly.

Milo walked out of the closet into the broad open expanse before them. "This … is the Hub," he said, arms open wide to include everything they could see. "The Hub exists everywhere and nowhere. As far as we can tell, it touches all universes, but is a part of none of them."

They were standing in a seemingly endless field with a tightly manicured lawn beneath their feet, the grass as tidy and trimmed as that of a golf course. The area looked like an outdoor science lab. Dozens of laboratory tables, covered in the equipment and detritus of ongoing experiments, were arranged in neat rows to the left. Dozens more tables were lined up in an array straight in front of them, each weighed down by computers and massive monitors. The monitors buzzed busily with graphs, charts, tables, moving lines, dots on grids, vast fields of text, and visions that were completely beyond the visitors' comprehension. Much of what they saw had no wires attached, but occasional cables from some equipment led to plugs directly in the grass below the tables. At one end, a printer was producing a three-dimensional model of what looked like a planet, though definitely not Earth. To the right were what appeared to be huge panes of glass, hanging in the air with no visible supports holding them from above or below. Resembling nothing so much as screens used to track people and information from some futuristic police station in a TV crime show, more graphs and charts flashed animatedly in bright red, blue, green, and yellow across these panes. The whole of the laboratory area was surrounded by a stone walkway, with stones of various sizes and hues interlaid into intricate patterns of swirls, bringing to mind the wind, or waves, or perhaps the movement of the galaxies.

Emma, Charlie, and Ben gawked in awe and amazement. "In the Hub," Milo continued with pride, "Everything is possible. Everything. Our scientists have been working here about ten years, some of them even living here, in which time they've created everything you see."

"What do you mean, 'they created everything'?" Emma asked Milo. She had a feeling he didn't mean "built."

"Power of intention," said Milo. "It works here." He shrugged.

"Well," said Charlie, "Not to be rude but I guess I'll be the one to bring up the elephant in the room." And he meant it in the most literal sense. Off to their left, about fifty yards beyond the stone path, an elephant munched quietly on a random patch of tall grass. Not just a normal elephant: this one seemed to be a two-dimensional life-sized actualization of a drawing, the kind a kindergartener might have made during art class. When it turned its head to look at them, they could see it was truly paper thin.

"That's Dr. Waldo's pet," Milo said, waving at a middle-aged man in a white lab coat who was approaching them in a great rush. "Dr. Waldo!" he said as the man drew near. "So good to see you!" The two men hugged.

"No time, no time!" said Dr. Waldo, breathless from the run

though he looked quite fit. "We've found a trail! You must go immediately! Who are these people?" His face registered surprise as he finally realized Eve and Milo were not alone.

Milo looked at the Earthlings. "New friends," he said, "but friends who we're going to have to leave behind. Sorry, guys, we can't take you with us. We have to go."

Emma was stunned. What had just happened? What kind of trail had Dr. Waldo found, and how were they going to follow it?

Ben's face fell. "Will we ever see you guys again? If you find Vik, will you come back and say goodbye?"

Eve looked at Ben and held his gaze. "I hope we see you again," she said, "I would like that." She looked back at Charlie and Emma. "You're staying at Ed Brooks's cabin, right?"

Charlie looked pleased but surprised. "How do you know?"

"We've been around a while," said Eve.

chapter five

"And then, they sent us home," Charlie finished. He, Emma, and Ben had been "unceremoniously rejected," as Charlie had put it, after Dr. Waldo told Milo and Eve he had "a hit." All three had returned to the twins' cabin to try to make sense of what had just happened.

When they got back to the cabin, they found Emma and Charlie's parents there, as well as Ed and his wife Ruby. While at the potluck, the twins' father, Glen, had told Ed about a leak in the cabin's back bathroom. Ed and Ruby had come over to fix it.

"I came over to *watch* Ed fix it," Ruby had corrected.

By the time the teens reached the cabin, the leak was fixed, and everyone was sitting in the living room chatting. Charlie, Emma, and Ben joined them, and Charlie recounted their rather unbelievable tale.

"That's the craziest thing I ever heard," said Ed when Charlie finished, "and I've seen some crazy things. But they confirmed my UFO story, did they? I was right? Not making it up? Not insane?" He squeezed Ruby, who was sitting at his side. "See, my love, you didn't marry a mad man, after all!"

Ruby rolled her eyes. "I'm not sure the UFO story was the only thing in question as far as your sanity," she laughed. "And I'm not sure I believe those people are from another planet. Anyway, we should probably be heading—"

There was a knock at the front door.

"Who in the world? At this hour?" said the twins' mother, Amy Renee, as their father got up.

Emma looked at a clock on the wall. It was nearing midnight.

Glen opened the door.

There stood the aliens.

"Eve!" said Ben and Charlie.

"Milo?" said Emma.

Amy Renee, who had joined her husband at the door, looked from the people standing in the doorway to her children and back. "So you're the aliens then?" she said matter-of-factly, as though people claiming to be aliens appeared on her doorstep every day. "I'm not so sure I should let you in."

"Let them in!" called Ed from the couch before Milo and Eve had a chance to reply. "I have questions!" Ruby elbowed him in the ribs, but nonetheless looked like she might have some questions herself.

"You're back!" said Charlie with great ebullience, as though he hadn't just seen them less than an hour before.

"You weren't gone long," said Emma, who hadn't even had time to start to miss Eve. Then she noticed something. "But … you changed your clothes again?" she said, half to herself. Which made her wonder, just where did Milo and Eve live? Where did they eat, sleep; where did they go to rest and recuperate and shower? Where did they keep their clothes? Did they live in the Hub? Emma and Charlie and Ben had been in the Hub for such a brief time that she hadn't had much time to look around before Dr. Waldo rushed everyone away, shoved Ben and Emma and Charlie back through the closet to the other side, to Earth. Not that they'd ever really left Earth, though she wasn't quite clear on how that all worked.

Eve looked down at her outfit, as though just noticing it herself. "Yes, I guess we did. We were gone longer than it seems," she said. "It was about a week, maybe. It's hard to tell sometimes. Anyway, we showered back at the Hub before we came over. We didn't get much chance to clean up for a few days." She squinched her nose. "Dad didn't smell so good."

Milo squinched his nose back at his daughter in reply. "We got pretty grungy this trip. I'm not the only one who didn't smell so good," he said. "But I won't tell the cute boys about your stench!"

At this, Amy Renee laughed. She extended her hand to Milo. "I'm Amy Renee. The twins' mother. This is my husband Glen."

"Milo, Eve," said Milo, indicating himself and his daughter in turn. They exchanged handshakes with the Nelsons. "We did a lot of running this time around," Milo continued. "Ended up on a very young planet, relatively speaking. No intelligent life. Just some fast creatures looking for a quick meal. We were almost dinner." He pulled up his pant leg to reveal a shin tightly wrapped in gauze. "Occupational hazard," he said.

"Hey, welcome. I'm Ed, and this is my wife Ruby," said Ed as the group moved to the living room and sat down. Milo nodded and smiled in greeting. "Just what is your occupation, there, Milo?" asked Ed. "Indiana Jones?"

Milo tilted his head in confusion. "Indiana Jones?"

Ed laughed. "Well, if you don't know Indiana Jones you're clearly not from here! Movie action adventure hero. A dashing archaeologist who gets himself caught up in all sorts of danger, but he always finds a way out."

Milo's eyes lit up. "An archaeologist action hero? Who would have imagined! Well, fact is, we never know what we're going to meet out there, and it keeps us on our toes, to say the least. Dr. Waldo—did they explain to you who Dr. Waldo is?" he paused.

Ed nodded. "We heard all about Dr. Waldo and The Grand Inconceivable Hub, or at least as much as they found out. Sounds like they weren't there long."

"No, I suppose not," said Milo, an enigmatic look on his face. "Well, Dr. Waldo tries to help keep us safe when we travel, but there's really not a lot he can do about it. The universes are largely empty, but there are a lot of wild places. You here on Earth, at this time in the planet's lifespan, you have it easy, more or less. You've made it pretty tranquil for yourselves. But in general, there's more that is uninhabitable and unfavorable to life out there than there is calm."

"A lot of peace, though," Eve added. "Lots of beautiful places with just nothing but serenity."

Emma found herself momentarily jealous. A life of quiet tranquility, rather than this chaos that normally surged through her head? She might be able to put up with some wild to get that in return.

Ruby, however, was caught up in the idea of time. "A week!" she said. "But the kids just got here an hour ago! How does that even work?" The furrow in her brow suggested she, too, was a skeptic.

"Time is a tricky concept," said Milo. "It's not as simple as people want to think it is. Don't believe me? Your people can send humans to the moon, but you can't keep the proper time on your clocks. Have you ever wondered why that is?"

As Ed nodded knowingly at her side, Ruby replied, "Yes, I guess I have, actually. Every time daylight savings changes, my car clock has run forward again by five or ten extra minutes. And the clock on our DVR doesn't even try to get it right. If I reset it, it's anyone's guess as to how long it'll be before it makes up its own time again, usually several decades into the future."

Milo's head bobbed up and down quickly. "Yes," he said, a gleam of excitement in his eyes. "Time! Time is slippery. It's not linear. People think it is, want it to be, expect it to be, and are confused when it's not. But time doesn't like to behave. Time envies the dimensions of space, which aren't expected to adhere to such strict rules. Time doesn't like being tied down. Time is your mischievous friend. Time wants to play."

"Time wants to play?" said Amy Renee. Emma could see her mother was having difficulty wrapping her head around the idea, around all of it. And Emma couldn't blame her. How could time not be linear, and what did that even mean? If it wasn't linear, then did it exist all at once, like space did? Did that mean that somewhere—in some other time? or place?—she could see her future, could know how all this would end up? They'd been studying free will in school; if all of time existed at once, could there be any such thing as free will?

Ruby looked very intently at Milo. "Seriously, are you telling me my husband isn't crazy? That UFO he claims he saw—it really was a UFO?"

"Well, that depends on how you define a UFO," said Milo. "In the strictest sense, it was an unidentified flying object. But Dr. Waldo suspects those sightings, or at least some of them, may have been disruptions resulting from Vik's attempts to unravel the thin spot—" he looked at Ruby. "Did they tell you about Vik, and the thin spots?"

Ruby nodded.

"Well, it may have been something Vik did, then. Or Ed could have been seeing through to another universe, maybe another planet's form of an airplane. Who knows. Hard to tell. What we've realized, though, is that Vik has been here for a long time. We can't find him, we keep trying, but we're almost certain he's been here."

"Why here?" asked Amy Renee. "Of all the places we could have

chosen to vacation! Why did this man come here? Is he dangerous?"
Emma could see her mother's mind whirling, starting to mentally
pack up the cabin and take them all back home.

Milo pursed his lips, gave some thought before speaking. "It's
close to home, relatively speaking. His elevator is your elevator.
First thin spot he found, I suppose." He looked out the window,
curtains still open, to the world beyond, blanketed in darkness.
"Earth has special interest to him," he said.

Emma had been watching the flurry of activity in a bit of a daze.
It didn't escape her attention that Milo had avoided the question
of whether Vik was dangerous. She remembered, though, that she
and Charlie and Ben had been dismissed from the Hub because Eve
and Milo were going on a mission. There had been a "hit." A "trail."

"Did you find him?" she asked. "Did you find Vik?"

All heads turned to Milo and Eve for the answer.

Milo's smile faded. "No. No, we didn't. We're new at this. It's an
imperfect science. One person in all the universes, it's a bit worse
than finding a needle in a haystack. We didn't find him, but we
didn't find any evidence that he'd been any of the places we went,
either." He looked at Eve. "We'll keep looking."

Emma wasn't sure if she was disappointed or glad. If they'd found
Vik, Milo and Eve might not have come back. Not that she needed
them to come back. But she wanted another look at the Hub. She
still wasn't fully sure she and the others hadn't been suffering from
some sort of mass delusion that made them think they'd seen a
giant room with a paper elephant grazing on grass, inside the lighthouse. That was impossible! "Everything is possible in the Hub,"
they'd told her, but she suspected the same might be true of hallu-
cinogenic trips. Or maybe all of it was a dream. Maybe she wasn't
even awake yet. She knew she needed to get back to the lighthouse
and find out.

"Eve," she said, "You told us you have some sort of 'master key' that unlocked the elevator—the storage room—at the lighthouse. Can we see your key?"

Once again, Eve looked at her father for approval. He shrugged. "Why not?" he said.

Eve reached to her neck and pulled out a pendant that had been resting underneath the neckline of her light blue shirt. "This is it," she said.

Emma stepped up to inspect the pendant. *It's nothing more than a small rock,* she thought. Her forehead wrinkled and the corners of her mouth tightened with displeasure.

Ruby leaned in to see, as well. "That's a wishing rock!" she said. "What kind of key is this? It's a wishing rock! Are you saying wishing rocks are keys to the universe?"

Emma was grateful that at least one other person—one other Earthling—was feeling the same disbelief she was. First, aliens from another universe. Now, common rocks unlocking doors to spaces between universes, where everything was possible. This was all too much.

"Not all wishing rocks are keys," Eve said. "Just some of them. But yes, the master key—at least, this one—looks like your wishing rocks, the kind your town is named after. A gray rock with a solid white stripe through it. They're like master keys. Using one is sort of primitive, actually; Dr. Waldo and his team have figured out the properties within the rock, the energy fields, that unlock things, and they've managed to replicate it. More or less. But I don't want to trust a duplicate. If we're going around the universes, I don't want to get stuck somewhere because Dr. Waldo missed something. It's the real rock for me."

Milo pulled out a similar pendant, hanging on a leather cord, from under his own shirt. "Me as well. No offense to Dr. Waldo.

He's safe in the Hub. We're out there getting chased by alien creatures that are looking for dinner. No leaving this to chance."

Ben reached out to the rock around Eve's neck. He asked a question with his eyes: "May I touch it?" Eve nodded yes. Ben gently lifted the rock, turned it over, looked closely.

"Just a rock," he said. "How do you know which wishing rocks are master keys and which aren't?" He released the rock, and it fell gently back to Eve's chest.

"The first time," Milo said, "it was an accident, as with many discoveries. We have these rocks on our planet, too. A woman—Eve's great great aunt, actually—was carrying one in her pocket near an elevator on our planet. Not an elevator exactly like your elevators, but the same general idea, anyway. The rest, as you all say, is history. Luckily she was a scientist. Her curiosity was piqued. She studied the rock to see what, if anything, made it different from other rocks, and then created a test to discern a 'master key' rock from other rocks. You still have to find the rocks before you can test them. They're hidden all over the universes, we're discovering."

"We have a bowl of wishing rocks in our house," said Ruby, shaking her head. "Lots of people in Wishing Rock do. There's a bowl full in this cabin, even, isn't there, Ed?"

"I think so," said Ed, and Amy Renee nodded slightly in recognition. She had seen the bowl of rocks, too.

"Are you saying some of those might be keys?" Ruby asked.

"Might be!" said Milo. "Everything is possible."

Ruby looked at Ed, eyes filled with incredulity. This was all a bit beyond belief.

"We have a couple bowls of wishing rocks, too," said Ben. "Does Dr. Waldo have a ... a rock-testing station, I guess, in the Hub? Could we bring all our rocks there to test them, see if any of them will unlock the universe?"

"Universes," said Charlie, nodding. "Plural."

Ben looked at Eve. "Weird that it's plural. Universes."

"I suppose, in theory, you could." Milo frowned. "It feels a little like cheating, though."

"Cheating how?" asked Emma. It didn't seem like cheating to her. What seemed like cheating was having a whole Hub at one's disposal, and arbitrarily deciding who could and couldn't get in. *That* seemed unfair. It wasn't *their* Hub. Obviously, it belonged to everyone, or no one, but it wasn't just theirs. She folded her arms across her chest.

"Cheating, like, maybe you're supposed to wait until the universes reveal themselves. You're not supposed to force it. I'm not saying I know that's how it is, but it seems it could be, doesn't it? Things happen when they're supposed to," said Milo.

"If that's the case," argued Emma, "then maybe this is how we're supposed to find out. Or maybe it's all just random anyhow. If you have a way to test wishing rocks, and your friend Vik has come here and disrupted our world with earthquakes and who knows what else, then it seems only fair that we get to travel around the universes too, if we can find the keys."

Hearing herself say those words, the reality of them hit Emma. The Hub was one thing. Another planet was another thing. Traveling through universes? It was almost more than her brain could handle.

"Well," said Eve, "some people think maybe we don't even need the rocks. The brain is an amazing thing." Her cheeks grew pink. "I mean, our brains are different from yours. I'm sure yours are just as advanced. But I'm talking about our brains. Dr. Waldo thinks our brains might not need the rocks. Yours, well, he hasn't studied that, as far as I know."

Emma felt like a specimen. "Dr. Waldo has been studying us?"

A big grin spread across Milo's face. "Oh yes! He finds you all fascinating. He has a particular love for British television, the British accent. That show where the blue police booth flies through space, he loves that. He's picked up on quite a few British phrases, as well as American, I'd say, though I'm not sure he always knows whether he's using them right. He got the Hub all hooked up to tap into various television stations around your world, especially over there in the UK. When he has time off, he watches. He's even taken to having himself a little tea time in the afternoon."

A swirl of questions formed in Emma's mind. "The afternoon," Milo said with such ease—but whose afternoon? How was time measured in the Hub? Did Milo and Eve's planet have multiple countries, just like Earth? With multiple languages and accents? And not the least of all this was the question of why these aliens looked so very human-like; was that normal? Did "intelligent life" mean "human-like form"?

"So what happens now?" asked Ed, interrupting Emma's thoughts. "You didn't find this guy. Do you keep looking?"

"We keep looking," said Milo with a deep sigh. "We don't know what he could do. He's not entirely himself right now. We need to return him home."

Ruby shook her head. "Did your government agree to that? I mean, are you just vigilantes? How do we know he's not the good guy in this scenario? How do we know he's not here to save us from you?"

Milo shrugged his shoulders. "You don't. I'd ask you to trust us, but we don't need your trust. We just need to do our job. Vik is a danger to many beings, and we're trying to stop him. That's all there is to it."

"Will you stay here, on our island?" asked Ed.

"We'll look around this place and time for a bit longer," said

Milo, "then jump forward a bit. Jumping forward in time is easier than backward, at least with the technology and knowledge we've gained so far, so we're moving forward in time slowly, trying to find evidence that Vik has been around. When we need to, we'll travel backward in time. Dr. Waldo is convinced that Vik has reason to be here, on your Earth, or has been here at some point in time, but he can't quite pinpoint it yet. So we continue our search."

"Can we search with you?" Charlie blurted out the question, but from the eager look on Ben's face it was clear the idea had been on his mind, too.

Amy Renee and Glen looked at each other. Their faces were easy to read, as well.

"No," said Glen. "Sorry kids, you can't."

Ben looked at Ed and Ruby with defiance, as though they'd spoken and denied him the opportunity. "I'm eighteen. I can make my own decisions," he asserted.

Ed looked at Ruby, who was frowning, and back to Ben. "Not up to us," he said. "But I'd hope you'd at least talk it over with your parents. Traveling the universe … universes … is a big deal, in a way." He looked back to Ruby. "Uh, I don't suppose I get to go either, do I?"

She stared him down. "No, you do not. We are newlyweds. We just got married. You can't go off to Mars. You need to stay here, with me."

Ed nodded. He looked at Milo. "You married?"

"Not really," said Milo. "It's complicated." He offered no further explanation.

"Lucky you," said Ed. Ruby punched him in the shoulder. "I was talking to myself, Rubes! I swear! Lucky me! I am lucky to be married to the most wonderful gal in all the universes! An opportunity to travel space and time is nothing compared to the opportunity to

spend all my days with Ruby Parker Brooks! Lucky me, lucky me!"
He grabbed Ruby around the waist and nuzzled a big kiss into her
neck. "Lucky me, lucky me!"

"Okay, okay!" said Ruby, laughing now. "You're forgiven."

"You know," said Milo to Ed, "Maybe you could help me search
here on Earth. If the others want to go along with Eve, I trust her."
His words indicated all the teens, but he looked only at Ben. "She's
been at this long enough. She knows what she's doing, and Dr.
Waldo will be in the Hub to help her with anything she needs."

"Are you kidding me?" said Amy Renee. "Charlie and Emma are
only seventeen. They're staying home. Sorry, kids."

"Come on, Mom," said Emma, who had realized the implications of Ben going off with Eve, without them. "We're almost eighteen. This is like a really intense science class! Think of how much
we'll learn! They don't teach this in school! You wouldn't deny us
that, would you?"

"I would and will and do," said Amy Renee. "And you're not almost eighteen; you just turned seventeen last month. Sorry, kiddos.
Earth it is for you."

"Well, I'm going," said Ben. "Eve, when do we leave? Where do
we begin?"

Eve glanced up at Ben with a mix of excitement and admiration.

Charlie saw the glance.

Emma saw the glance.

Charlie and Emma exchanged a look: there was no way Ben and
Eve were going off without them.

chapter six

Two days later, after Ed and Milo had eaten breakfast with the Nelsons, they'd gone off in search of any sign of Vik on the island. Ed had enlisted Wishing Rock's resident psychic to see if she had any suggestions as to where they might look. Fascinated by the prospect, the woman had tried her best, but was not able to tune her abilities to the matter at hand. Still, she did suggest that they head to the less-explored northwest part of the small island. With nothing better to go on, Ed and Milo had donned sturdy hiking shoes, packed up their rucksacks, and headed off in Milo's old truck to parts more or less unknown.

After the men left the cabin, while the Nelson parents were busy putting the kitchen back in order after the morning meal, Charlie and Emma exchanged another look: now was the time.

Emma grabbed the backpacks they'd covertly packed the day before. Charlie filled bottles of water for them in the kitchen. "Going on a bike ride," he said to their mother, who was just closing up the dishwasher with the morning's dirty dishes. He and Emma ran off before she could say a word.

It was true. They were going on a bike ride. At least, that's how the day was going to start.

They whipped at maximum speed along the winding road to the

lighthouse, where they first leaned their bikes against a short log fence that separated the path to the building from the parking lot.

"But what if someone sees them?" said Emma.

"There's nothing wrong with our bikes being at the lighthouse," said Charlie.

Emma had to agree; technically no one had told them they couldn't go to the lighthouse. Still, she moved her bike around to the back side of the lighthouse, and partially hid it behind a bush. Charlie followed suit without objection.

Inside, they approached the storage room.

The day before, Emma had gathered a handful of small wishing rocks at the beach. She didn't hold out much hope that one of them might, by some random chance, be a master key to the universe, but seeing as they had no other key, no other way to get inside, she and Charlie had decided they may as well try. Drawing the stones out of her pocket, Emma waved them randomly in front of the door.

Nothing happened.

She tried again. Still nothing.

"Let me try," said Charlie. Emma handed over the rocks, wondering what it was about people that made them think *their* doing something might make it work, when someone else's doing it hadn't. It's not as though Charlie had any more knowledge about the rocks than she had. It's not as though Charlie could differentiate a wishing rock that was a key to the universe from one that wasn't. They'd each only gotten the briefest look at Eve's necklace, and Emma suspected Charlie's attention had not been entirely on the rock that hung from Eve's neck, as much as it may have been on what it lay on.

Still, if there was any chance that he might figure out something she hadn't—

The storage room door opened.

Charlie gasped.

"What did you do? Which one did you use?" asked Emma.

"I just—" and he waved his hand, filled with rocks, in front of the door as he'd done moments before, in a random path through the air.

"That's the same thing I did," said Emma. Her face fell.

Charlie saw her disappointment at her own failure. "I also chanted 'aliens aliens aliens,'" he said. "Maybe that was it."

Emma raised her shoulders, then dropped them with a loud sigh. "Well, whatever you did, it worked. Let's go in before it closes."

They walked inside the small room, which was much less cramped this time, with only the two of them in there. The door closed behind them, and darkness filled the room. Even the light from the crack where the door was seemed to disappear.

"Did you happen to notice where the light switch was?" whispered Charlie. Emma knew he was standing right by her side, not two feet away, but she couldn't see even a shadow of him.

She shook her head "no," then realized he couldn't see her either. "No idea," she said. "So, what now?"

In the darkness Emma sensed movement and heard Charlie start up his soft chant again. "Aliens aliens aliens ..."

The door to the Hub opened. Emma and Charlie blinked rapidly as their pupils protested the sudden bright light.

"Of all the things in the universe," mumbled Emma, "and 'aliens aliens aliens' works."

"Universes," said Charlie. "Plural. I'm magic, I guess, Em. I've been telling you for years. I'm special" He stepped into the Hub, where Eve and Dr. Waldo stood, waiting, looks of great amusement on their faces.

"Special indeed," said Emma under her breath.

"Honeys, we're home!" called out Charlie, smiling back at Eve's effervescent grin as he approached the young woman. Her smile grew bigger.

"Welcome back!" laughed Dr. Waldo. "Good, good. We don't get many visitors. Delighted to have you here!"

Emma looked at the bespectacled man with his short gray hair. Charlie may have been convinced of his own magic, but Emma was not. "Dr. Waldo, how is it possible that Charlie managed to unlock the storage room? And the Hub? What did he do that I didn't do? It couldn't be the chant," she said. *It couldn't be.* Rather, not that it couldn't be, but Emma would have been disappointed with the universes if it were that simple.

"No, no, no, my dear," said Dr. Waldo, welcoming her and guiding her into the room with a gentle hand on her shoulder. "Of course not! Security cameras, you see. We have security cameras. We saw you coming. We opened the doors for you."

"Likely story," said Charlie, with a wink to Eve.

Did Eve blush? Emma thought maybe she had. Were all aliens quite so human-like? Emma wondered again, not sure if this would be a good thing or a bad thing. On the one hand, it would make things easier. She might have felt awkward having conversations with a giant talking lizard or a green blob with oversized eyes. Come to think of it, why were aliens so often depicted as green? Weren't they? Or was she just remembering wrong? Who really knew, anyway? But then, if aliens were, in fact, real, and living here, on Earth, or next to it in the Hub, however that worked, and if, in fact, there were elevators all around the Earth, a handful of them at least, a smattering of elevators, then it could well be that other people had truly encountered aliens before, couldn't it? There wouldn't need to be spaceships, apparently; there needn't have been UFOs. The question of the time it might take for aliens to even get to Earth became a moot point. Regardless of how long a spaceship might take to get to Earth, an elevator, apparently, took no time at all. Well, Emma thought, she didn't know that. She hadn't traveled in the elevator … yet.

She felt the pressure of the weight of her backpack on her back. It seemed so insufficient for the adventure they were hoping to embark on. Having no idea what one might take along to travel the universes, she and Charlie had decided on a change of clothes, socks, underwear, some granola protein bars, and toothbrushes. Emma had argued that they should take along extra pairs of shoes, but Charlie convinced her it would just be extra weight. The things Emma usually took along on trips—books, her iPod, some money—seemed superfluous. Emma, a great keeper of lists, had a master packing list from which she packed for all trips. However, things like playing cards and an umbrella seemed so out of place when packing for universal travel as to be ridiculous. When she'd gotten to "insect repellant" on her list, Emma had almost backed out of the excursion entirely.

"Insect repellant?" she'd said to Charlie, quietly. They'd been in her room at the cabin, him sitting on her bed and her on the floor, her empty plum-and-black backpack open before her. "Insect repellant!" she'd repeated. "Who knows what kind of repellant we'll need? What if there's a planet with mosquitoes the size of horses? What if there's a planet covered with spiders, Planet of the Spiders, angry spiders that can talk and kill?"

Charlie had shaken his head. "What someone needs to invent," he'd said, "is dangerous-alien repellent. Make note of that, please, to tell the committee."

"Noted," Emma had said.

Emma had not packed the insect repellant. What was the point? In the end, with so many unknowns, the options seemed to be either to bring everything and try to be prepared for every possible possibility (which was impossible), or to bring just the bare essentials, and wing it.

And so, they would wing it. If, that is, they even went anywhere.

Emma had, however, packed a notebook and pen for writing out her lists—she would have been lost without her notebook—and Charlie a tube of Chapstick, without which he would have felt something was missing. These went with them everywhere; part of the packing process. Notebook? Check. Chapstick? Check. Their packing, incomplete as it was, was done.

As Emma and Charlie were looking around the Hub, trying to take in everything they hadn't had time to notice before, the door from the storage closet opened again.

There stood Ben.

He, too, had a backpack on his shoulder, and a look of delight on his face that quickly transformed to confusion.

"Emma? Charlie?" he said, walking to the chair next to Eve and setting his backpack on it. "Here to … look around?" he asked. His tone was hesitant. Emma's mood deflated. Was he not happy to see her? Or maybe, she thought, he wasn't happy to see Charlie.

"Here to look around," said Emma quietly, "and maybe come along."

"Your parents gave you permission, then?" said Ben, looking at Charlie.

Charlie, bitterly aware that Ben had not technically had to ask for permission from his own parents, squirmed, but said nothing.

"When Eve and Milo showed up at the cabin, they said they'd been gone a whole week. But it seemed like just an hour or so to us. We figured we could, you know, come along, and just be sure to time it so we're back by dinnertime," said Emma. She turned to Dr. Waldo. "You can do that, right? You can finagle that?"

Dr. Waldo laughed. "Oh! Finagle! What a lovely word. Finagle! Finagle! It's a word that uses so many parts of the mouth, leaves no one out! Finagle! It should be an animal, really. Like an eagle, but more delicate. If I discover a flying creature that is not yet named, I shall call it a finagle. Hee hee!" Dr. Waldo danced a small jig of delight.

"But forgive me, friends!" he declared. "You're here now, we have no trails to follow, no one is leaving just yet! Last time you were here, we had to push you out the door before you could see a thing, that won't do, not good at all. A proper introduction to the Hub, then! I've been remiss, just standing here, let's have a look around, shall we? Ben saw a bit of the place already, but not all of it. Yes, the Grand Hub Tour, let's go!"

When was Ben here, and for how long? Emma wondered. Knowing he and Eve had spent time together, alone, was not reassuring to her at all. Maybe there was a way they could all travel the universes … without Eve?

"Well, then, where to begin," said Dr. Waldo, leading the way as they walked. "I'm the Hub's Primary Spotkeeper, you see, official title, one of many. We have quite a variety of scientists here from our planet, Lero, that's the name of our home planet, yes, working on numerous projects. Some are based here; some commute from home for work."

"They commute?" asked Charlie. "Like, on a bus? A subway?"

"On the elevator, obviously," said Emma, though however obvious it might be, it seemed impossible. "They just come for the day?"

"Why yes, it's as simple as commuting work is for anyone else," said Dr. Waldo. "We haven't yet figured out how our scientists can telecommute, as you call it, but we are working on it, we'll figure it out! We'll finagle a way! Yes, we will *finagle a way!*" He chuckled at himself and wiggled his hips a bit, a smaller, more contained version of his earlier dance, then deliberately regained professional composure. "Yes! Commuters, in the office for a few hours a day, sometimes for a few days. 'Days,' of course, being a subjective term. Time is so very tricky. How even to describe or define it? Still, we manage, we do, we've got it down to a science you could say, yes, down to a science!"

"Are you the lighthouse keeper, too, then?" asked Emma. "I'd think with so much activity going on in the closet, surely someone would notice?"

"Oh my, no," said Dr. Waldo. "That's the groundskeeper, he's a good friend, he's from Lero too, yes, we put together a resumé for him, got him the job here years ago, good man, no one really bothered to check his references, thank goodness. But no need, the storage room, as you call it, it's sound proof. When the door is closed, it fully seals itself, fills in all the molecules. No light or sound escapes from within. My, wouldn't that make a mess when traveling between universes, if molecules could leak out the door!" He tittered at the image and waved his hands in the air. "Bits and pieces of us all, scattered throughout the universes! No, better designed than that, better designed indeed, we can be quite thankful, to be sure!"

"Your planet, it's named Lero?" said Emma. She turned to Eve. "That's where you're from, too?"

Eve nodded. "Lero is home," she said.

"If the scientists can commute here, is that what you're doing too? Are you still living on Lero, sleeping there at night, searching for Vik during the day?" Emma asked.

Eve shook her head. "No. Our schedule is so crazy. We've mostly been sleeping in the Hub, in the cabins out back." She gestured vaguely at the distance off to her left. "But whenever one of the scientists gets a hit on Vik, we go. It's easier if we're here. Otherwise they'd have to come get us on Lero. Like Dr. Waldo said, we haven't figured out telecommuting yet, nor have we figured out how to make long distance calls from here to home." Emma and Charlie had debated bringing their phones with them—they felt somewhat naked without them—but had realized the futility of the idea. Strange that something so ubiquitous as a cell phone could be so useless outside the small confines of their own planet.

"Right she is," said Dr. Waldo, "quite right! Cell phones within one universe, well, that's just a matter of getting the signal to go the distance, you see, or folding the distance, one or the other; regardless, it's all together, isn't it? But jumping between universes, well, we haven't figured that one out just yet. Give it time, give me time! We shall conquer interuniverse communications, you will see!"

"Is the Hub here just to help you find Vik?" Charlie asked. "You guys must really want to find him."

"No, not at all," said Dr. Waldo. "The Hub is here because the Hub is here. We are here because we want to study the Hub and the universes. Milo and Eve are here because we need to find Vik. We are, as you people like to say, multitasking." He wiggled his eyebrows.

"You're determined," said Emma to Eve. "It doesn't sound like you have much to go on, but here you are."

"No, I suppose it doesn't," said Eve, but she offered nothing else. There was more to the story, Emma realized, but she had no clue what that could be.

"So, let's talk about that elephant, then," said Charlie. The elephant they'd seen on their first visit was still there, off in the general direction in which Eve had indicated the cabins were to be found. "What's up with the elephant?"

Dr. Waldo stammered a bit. "Well, yes, of course, not real science I suppose, but who's to say what is real science? There is more to the natural world than any of us realizes. When I first got here and learned I could manifest anything, I, well, I'd seen a show that day, an Earth show about elephants, and I suppose I just thought about it so much, didn't really know how the power of intention worked just yet, all the forces came together and there, you see, next thing I knew, there was an elephant in the room. A real one, that was. Not this flat drawing, but a real elephant. As you might imagine, we quickly learned that a science lab, large as ours might be, is no place for an elephant. Not the least of it was cleaning up after it." He shuddered at the memory. "So I un-imagined that one. But I am a fan of your idioms, you see, just as you say, the elephant in the room, I liked the idea of it, so I intentioned this one into existence." He looked fondly over at the giant two-dimensional creature. "I've named him Rupert. Mostly he grazes. He might be lonely. I wonder. I don't know for sure. One gets lonely when one is just one. I didn't know much about elephants when I created him, which is part of why I created him as a two-dimensional drawing rather than a live being. It seemed wrong to bring a creature here without really knowing much about its needs or thoughts or wishes. Rupert is flat, of course, but who's to say a flat elephant doesn't wish for company as much as a real one? Maybe I should make a companion for Rupert." His cheery mood had turned quite introspective. "Creating this space is quite a responsibility, ladies and gentlemen," he said. "It is not something to be taken lightly. Everything we do has an effect somewhere else. We may never see it or know it, but our actions have consequences. Always."

"The butterfly effect," said Emma. Seeing Eve's look of confusion, she added, "It's a saying we have. The idea that a butterfly flapping its wings somewhere might somehow cause a tornado on the other side of the world, just from one thing leading to another, I guess. I'm not sure exactly how it happens, but that's the saying."

Eve nodded her understanding.

"The butterfly effect!" repeated Dr. Waldo. "I do love your sayings. Yes, that is exactly it. The butterfly effect!"

The Hub—inside or outside, whatever it was—was just the right temperature, sunny but not too hot, only a few small puffy clouds high in the sky, with a gentle breeze blowing through every now and then, enough to tickle the skin but not so much as to disturb the lab notes sitting loose on the tables. The cheerful chirps of a variety of birds could be heard in a chorus, not too loud nor too quiet, and the sound of a river or maybe even a waterfall soothed from somewhere in the distance.

"Dr. Waldo," said Emma, "I hear birds but I don't see any. Are they hiding somewhere?"

"Clever! You are clever, young lady! No, well, I do like birds, of course, of course, nature is beautiful, is it not, but you see, when I designed an outdoor science lab, outdoors because I do like a good breath of fresh air, keeps the mind alert, but naturally it just wouldn't do to have birds defecating on my science, now would it? There are no birds here, just the birds' songs. You hear them but don't see them because they are only here to be heard, not seen. Brilliant! Everything is possible! Not that I don't like birds, let's be clear; they just don't mix with computers."

Dr. Waldo continued. "Now, let's explore my world here a bit, shall we?" Like a giddy child, he led them quickly toward another area of the Hub. They left the tidy grassy area on which the laboratory was set up (which led Emma to wonder: was the storage room inside the laboratory? Was the laboratory inside the storage room? Her mind could not quite grasp the idea), and walked across a small field of wildflowers, a fragrant blaze of magenta and rose and yellow and periwinkle in a bed of emerald green. Ahead of them loomed a large building which seemed to shimmer between visible and invisible. When it was visible, a large sign over the front could be seen: "Experimental Building."

Dr. Waldo seemed a bit sheepish but nonetheless animated. "When I was creating this building, I had the idea of an invisible building, but I couldn't quite decide how that would work. This was the result—wavering thoughts, wavering building. I've since learned more about how to direct the creation intention, but I suppose I enjoy watching the building go in and out of existence like that, reminds me we're all just temporary, you know, could disappear at any time. Don't worry, once we're inside it's all solid as can be, you won't notice a thing, it's just like this from the outside."

As they climbed the grand staircase to the oversized double-doored entry, the steps beneath them fluctuated in and out of visibility. When the steps were invisible, it seemed they were walking on air. Emma wished the stairs would stay invisible longer so she could savor the feeling that she was floating. Maybe one day, she thought, she'd have the chance to imagine a building of her own into existence here in the Hub. Would they allow that?

She paused. Would they allow that? The question itself implied something much greater. Once they found Vik, then what? Would they close off the Hub to Emma and Charlie forever?

"Is this all a secret?" she asked. "The Hub, is it a secret? Are we not supposed to know about it? Are we not supposed to be here?"

"Well, young lady, that's an interesting question, isn't it? The answer, my dear, is that I can't really say. We don't know. At any rate, it is not for we, the citizens of Lero, to decide. It's up to the universes. The universes reveal secrets in their own time, their own way. Sometimes it's a matter of whether people are ready to see it. There's a room in this building, for example, that you can only see if you're ready to see it. Otherwise you wouldn't know it even exists."

"What room is that?" asked Ben, voicing the thoughts of all the others. "What does it do? What's in it?"

To no one's surprise, Dr. Waldo didn't answer.

Instead, he led them through the front of the building to the interior. Just as he'd promised, once they were inside, the building ceased its hide-and-seek, and remained visible.

"This way!" he said, trotting down the wide, tiled hallway to the left. He stopped at the third door down on the right. With a mighty pleased look on his face, he said, "Welcome to the Secret Garden!"

Emma raised one eyebrow. "If you're telling us about it, it's not much of a secret is it? Not to mention the sign." She pointed over the door, where "The Secret Garden" was written in romantic, flowery script.

"Not that kind of secret," he said. With great flourish, he opened the door. Spread out before them, through the doorway, was a vast garden … outside.

"Outside?" said Charlie. "I'm confused. This is a door inside a building. How is the garden outside? Do these doors just lead to the outside again? This isn't a room. This is … outside."

"So you're saying we're outside, then?" Dr. Waldo asked gleefully. "Yes! Yes, you're correct! In the Experimental Building, in the Hub itself, *everything is possible*. A door doesn't have to lead to a room. It can just lead to another place. Here, the place is my Secret Garden. This is where secrets grow!" He leaned down to caress a fern-like plant. "One of the first secrets I planted here. It's doing well."

Emma thought she saw a brief shadow cross over the scientist's normally happy features. "You … plant secrets here?" she asked, looking around the garden. It was enormous, with hundreds if not thousands of plants. Did Dr. Waldo have that many secrets? How could one person possibly survive with so many secrets inside him?

Dr. Waldo shook his head. "Oh, no, no, these aren't all mine. Most of them just popped up on their own. I think the universes use this room too, unbeknownst to me, but with my blessing. The more the merrier! Plants just appear. The universes' magical and myriad secrets. They grow here. Sometimes when we make a discovery, I'll notice that a plant will disappear. Coincidence? I'm not sure. It's all a mystery. I created this garden to plant my one great secret, and a few others after that, but as you can see, the universes are quite full of secrets of their own." He turned to Eve. "Your father planted a secret here, once, did you know that?"

A cloud came over Eve's face and her lips pinched ever so slightly. "I didn't know that."

Emma got the feeling that Eve might know what the secret was. Looking around the room, she pondered all the secrets of all the worlds. Surely this garden, massive as it was, couldn't contain all of them. Were these the secrets of all the scientists? The secrets of people on Lero?

It seemed it would remain a mystery.

"How do you plant secrets, Dr. Waldo?" Emma asked.

"Good question, good question," he said. He pointed to the right, to a row of miniature houses. "Fairy houses, you might call them," he said. "You tell a fairy house your secret, and you wait. The fairy house decides what kind of plant your secret will be. The plant appears in a pot in front of the fairy house. Then you go over there—" he pointed at a shed Emma had not noticed before "—and get yourself a shovel, find a good place for the secret, and you plant it."

"You have to plant it yourself? It doesn't just … appear somewhere in the garden?" asked Charlie.

Dr. Waldo looked at Charlie, waggled his index finger in the air. "Keeping secrets takes work sometimes, you know."

He then walked back to the door back to the hallway. From the garden side, the door was just a door within a frame, unencumbered by surrounding walls, ceiling, or anything else, much like the door from the storage room to the Hub itself. A strange sight, thought Emma, but she suspected it would not be the strangest thing she saw today.

"Where to next?" asked Ben, his eyes wide as he took in the field. "This is fantastic!"

"I'll take you where I go to think," said Dr. Waldo. "But you'll have to stay with me. It's a room designed just for me, really." It was becoming clear to Emma that Dr. Waldo's Experimental Building was a place he went to exercise his creativity and indulge his sense of humor. While he was proud of his accomplishments, he may have been just a bit embarrassed by the seeming folly of the way he'd spent some of his time.

"Unlike the commuters," he said, as though he were reading Emma's thoughts, "I live here. I've lived here a long time. In my free time, well, I like to play. In a place where everything is possible, it is difficult not to test the limits sometimes."

"You said that before," said Charlie. "What do you mean, 'everything is possible'? How is that possible?"

"We're not entirely sure, Charlie, but what we believe is that the Hub is a combination of all the universes—it is within all the universes, separate from all of them, yet a part of all of them. In different universes, different things are possible. Here at the convergence of all possible points, when you combine all the possibilities of all the infinite universes, well, suddenly everything is possible. It's just a matter of learning how to work within the possibilities. The limitations are ours, not the Hub's."

They continued down the long hallway (impossibly long, thought Emma, based on the exterior size of the building), passing multiple rooms on the way, each with an intriguing name carved or written on a plaque over the door. "The Passage of Time." "Key to My

Heart." "Cloud Nine." "Square One." "Out on a Limb." "Blessing in Disguise." "The Funny Farm." "Musical Chairs." "In a Nutshell." The names captivated Emma's imagination, and she wanted to peek into each as they passed, but none of these was Dr. Waldo's destination. At one point they passed a room where the door had been blown out. "Never mind that," said Dr. Waldo dismissively as they walked by, never losing the glimmer of exhilaration in his eyes. "I was experimenting in there with a loose cannon, yes, didn't quite get it right just yet. Not quite yet." Finally he stopped. "Here we are," he said with a sigh of contentment.

The script over this door was brief: "Thought."

"I wonder what we'll find today?" he said enigmatically. Opening the door, he skipped inside.

It was impossible to see much beyond the entrance, as everything past five feet inside the door was blocked by a hedge of boxwood, taller by far than Dr. Waldo or any of the others.

Dr. Waldo smiled at the look of confusion on the teens' faces. "It's a maze," he explained, as though it were the most obvious thing in the world. "I come here to literally get Lost in Thought. Stay with me," he warned. He gently caressed the green wall in front of him; it looked tidy and compact, as though it had just been trimmed. "Some days I follow the left side, and some days I follow the right side," he said, keeping his left hand extended to the hedge, his fingertips reading the small, glossy leaves like braille, as he walked along the path between hedges.

"What does it lead to?" asked Charlie, following closely behind Dr. Waldo.

Dr. Waldo shrugged with glee. "It changes every time. That is the best thing about being Lost in Thought. The unexpected revelations that surprise and delight you. Turn a corner in Thought, and who knows what you'll discover?"

Emma had to agree with this assessment, but she was confused about the creation of this room. "How does Thought change every time, without your changing it? How does it change on its own?" she asked.

"Yes, yes, good question, Emma, good question! It's all part and parcel with how I built Thought. I wanted the room to crawl into my mind, get into the crevices, see the things I was not seeing, and then show them to me. The room, simply stated, reads my mind and reveals to me the things that are there, but which I have somehow hidden from myself. The things where, as you Earthlings might say, I have two here and two there but have not yet put them together to make four. The Thought room is a tangible manifestation of my brain. You are, in essence, inside my brain right now!" As Dr. Waldo said this, joyful, bouncy music suddenly erupted around them, coming out of nowhere. Dr. Waldo grabbed Emma's hand and twirled her about. "We are dancing in my brain!" He laughed and wove around the others in a quick do-si-do, then as the music subsided (but still, somehow, lingered, as though the hedge was humming it in its mind), Dr. Waldo's left hand found the hedge again, and he resumed his walk through the maze.

Ben, however, was still stopped in his tracks. "The room reads your mind?" he said, his brows bunched in skepticism. "That's impossible. How can a room read your mind?"

Dr. Waldo laughed. "Young man," he said. "Young man."

Ben waited for Dr. Waldo to continue, but when the older man said nothing, Ben said, "Yes? Young man what?"

"Young man. Do you understand the word 'everything'?"

"Yes?" Ben said.

"Do you understand the word 'possible'?"

Ben gave a shrug that indicated his frustration with this line of questioning. "Of course, yes?"

"Then is it the word 'is' that is troubling you?"

"I don't understand the question."

"'Everything is possible.' We discussed this, my friend! 'Everything is possible in the Hub.' We are in the Hub. Hence and therefore, everything is possible here. If it's possible anywhere, then it's possible here too."

"Are you saying there are worlds where mind reading is possible?" asked Emma.

"Well, of course! Everything is possible somewhere. There are planets where people can read minds, simple as can be, it's just a matter of the wavelengths, their brains are calibrated to read brain wavelengths just as sure as your phone is calibrated to read phone wavelengths. That's simplifying it, of course, but you understand. On our planet, our vision is very different from yours. As you know, your eyes can only see a very small part of the full spectrum of light. Ours see things you perhaps did not imagine could be seen. We can see the spirits of the dead, or at least, those who have chosen to stick around."

"'Those who have chosen to stick around?'" asked Charlie. "They have a choice?"

Dr. Waldo nodded vigorously. "Oh, of course! On your planet as well as on ours. Some stick around, some move on."

Emma thought about her grandfather, who had died two years before. He had been her favorite, with the tall tales he'd spun for the enjoyment of his grandchildren, his laugh, hardly a sound but more of a full-body expression of mirth. Was he still here on Earth … or rather, outside the lighthouse door, on Earth?

"If they move on, where do they go?" she asked.

"We don't know where all of them go, but we have discovered there's a whole universe made up, as far as we can tell, of planets filled with nothing but spirits—ghosts, if you will. Spirits from all universes. They don't all seem to go there, but many do. It's quite a menagerie! A melding of so many universes! I can well imagine why a spirit, released from its planetary reigns, would want to go there. Imagine being able to talk with beings from all the universes, without hardly having to leave your own backyard!"

The way he spoke, Emma imagined ghosts holding a massive barbecue, alien creatures of every type, size, shape, every imaginable being, streaming in and out the sliding glass door out back, filling up red picnic cups with punch or wine. Did ghosts eat?

While Emma was lost in thoughts of her own, Dr. Waldo continued with a litany of different universes and planets. "There are planets where you can turn invisible," he said. "Planets with different gravity where people can fly. Planets, as I was saying, where brain waves are more tangible, allowing beings to read each others' minds. Planets where people—I use the term people for ease of understanding, of course—planets where people can fold space as easily as I can fold a piece of paper, making travel a mere logistical technicality. There's a whole universe for Lost and Broken Things— lost pens, lost socks, lost time, broken hearts, broken promises, even lost souls, oh, yes. Visiting that universe is only for the courageous and compassionate, that's for certain. And a universe for Things Left Unsaid. Dense universe, that, so many planets, sad sad place, never want to go there again. There are planets—"

But Emma was still thinking about the spirits. "Dr. Waldo," she said, hardly realizing she was interrupting him, "Can we visit the ghost universe?"

The spritely old man stopped and shivered visibly. "My goodness. Well, yes, of course, but …" He muttered something so quietly that Emma couldn't hear, then continued, more loudly, "Well, it's dangerous. People who stay there too long can't return. Dangerous. No, no, not a good idea. Best leave death for the dead. We all will get there soon enough." He continued to mumble under his breath, but Emma couldn't make out any further words.

They'd been walking only about ten minutes, but with another turn around another corner, the front door to the room suddenly appeared before them again, "Exit" emblazoned and flashing above the frame.

"We're done?" said Charlie. He nudged Dr. Waldo. "Not much on your mind today, eh, Waldo?"

"Oh, to be sure, to be sure, much on my mind, Charlie! Very much! The room knew that I need to get back to work, that's what's on my mind, so today it didn't let me get too lost. Back to the laboratory I must go! But you kids feel free to look around, if you're not meant to be somewhere it won't let you in, no worries! I designed it that way, you see, easier than keys, all about intention. And one must trust the universes, yes, sometimes someone is meant to be somewhere, meant to discover something, unbeknownst to me. If it were left to me I wouldn't give them the key, of course, you understand? But the universes will let them go where they need to go. Everything in its time, everything as it's meant to be, such beautiful, unimaginable, chaotic order!"

With that, they exited Thought and headed back toward the laboratory.

"Dr. Waldo," said Emma, "can you explain to us who the … uh … elevator, how it works, exactly? What it does?"

Dr. Waldo flung his arms wide to include all the universes in an embrace. "Who knows, my child, who knows?"

Emma felt both flabbergasted and a bit annoyed. Here this man had been talking as though he knew everything, and yet he didn't even know how the elevators worked? "You mean you don't know at all?"

"We know a little," he said. "We are scientists. We're here to study the elevators, as well as many other things. We have ideas, hypotheses as to how the elevators work, we're striving to figure it all out, but we don't know everything."

"Well, what *do* you know?"

"We know that there are keys, like the one Eve showed you as well as other kinds of keys, strewn throughout the universes, keys that access both places and possibilities. Sometimes the keys work without your doing a thing, and sometimes you need to give them a mental nudge, let them know what you want. The universes have given us keys, indeed, but still it seems the universes are not without their own agendas."

Ben reached to his neck and pulled out the wishing rock that was resting on his chest at the end of a long cord. "Keys like this one," he said. Emma felt a wave of envy for Ben and Eve's matching pendants.

Dr. Waldo nodded.

"You said there are keys that access both places and possibilities. What do you mean? How do you access a possibility?" asked Emma.

Eve held out her wrist. "This bracelet," she said, indicating a brushed metal band around her wrist, embedded with a variety of stones, "isn't just jewelry. Each of these stones does something. This is a part of our 'travel pack.' I'd be lost if I lost this bracelet, because these stones help us travel where we need to go. For example, this one," she pointed to a stone that looked like an extremely clear crystal quartz, "is a translation stone. I speak more English now, but when we got here, I didn't know much. The stone helped."

"How did it help?" asked Charlie, reaching to hold Eve's fingers, gently turning her wrist so he could get a closer look at the bracelet. It was a little more than half an inch wide, and fit snugly but comfortably around Eve's wrist, fastened by some well-hidden latch.

Eight small, different stones were securely spread out along the full
width of the band, with narrow strips of the same brushed metal
crossing over the stones to ensure they wouldn't fall out.

"It ... well, it translates, that's it, really. It makes it so the person talking and the people listening can understand each other,
without even realizing they're not all speaking the same language.
It translated my speech to English, and it translated other people's
English to my language so I could understand."

"It translates ... like, into your ear? Into your head?" asked Ben.

"I guess into the air, maybe? It changes the sound waves into the
sound waves of a different language, that's the best I can describe it."

"Trippy," said Charlie.

Eve pointed to another rock embedded on the bracelet. This
stone resembled amber, and seemed to have a tiny air bubble
trapped inside the center. "This one creates a sort of atmospheric
shield around you if it's needed, so you can breathe. We don't know
if it's permanent or if it only lasts a few hours—we haven't tested
that out yet. But on the occasions where we've landed on planets
where the atmosphere might not be compatible with us, it kept us
alive until we were able to leave. As far as we know, it could work
indefinitely, but we hope we don't have to find out the hard way
that we're wrong."

"You guys say 'as far as we know' a lot," said Charlie. "Do you not
know very far?"

"It's science, sir," said Dr. Waldo, taking off his wire-rimmed
glasses and studying the glass. Finding a speck, he wiped the glasses
on his lab coat and returned them to his face. "We are learning. We
don't know everything, by far, yet. In fact, it's likely that with all
there is to know, we hardly know anything. The greatest and most
challenging part of the pursuit of truth, young Charlie, is learning
to embrace uncertainty. If we couldn't, we could never learn. We'd

be immobilized, insisting our ideas were impenetrably correct, and we'd stagnate. One thing we've observed about Earthlings, people on your planet have become far too enamored of certainty. Clinging to it like a parasite. It will tear you apart, if you all don't learn to welcome uncertainty again. We've seen it happen, on our mother planet."

"Your mother planet?" started Ben, but by then the group had reached the laboratory, near the entrance from the elevator, where people they'd not seen before were buzzing all around the computers and screens. It looked as though some of the computers had been disturbed somehow; a few people were righting tables and chairs.

A tall brunette woman in a white lab coat rushed over. "Dr. Waldo, we just had a small quake. Did you not feel it? Here, in the Hub. A quake. Vik must be near. Eve must leave now. We've found a trail! We have another hit!"

chapter seven

Dr. Waldo spun to face Eve, who was nodding before he even said anything. "No time to waste! Hurry!" Eve started to run off but saw another scientist racing to meet her, carrying Eve's bag and jacket. Eve slipped her arms into her jacket, grabbed her bag, and quickly re-joined the group.

Turning next to Ben, Dr. Waldo grabbed him by the shoulders and looked him sternly in the eyes. "Are you sure you're ready, young man? Do you understand what you're up against? This could be very dangerous. Are you ready?"

Ben radiated nervous excitement. "I'm ready! Where's my backpack?" He looked around aimlessly, found his pack where he'd left it earlier by the elevator, and picked it up. "What do we do?" His anticipation was almost palpable.

Charlie stepped forward. "We're going, too," he said firmly.

Eve, Ben, and Dr. Waldo stared at Charlie. Emma blushed, but straightened her back and moved closer to Charlie to show her solidarity. They were going, too.

"I don't know," said Eve, fidgeting with a closure on her bag. "I mean, your parents ..."

Dr. Waldo, agitated at the waste of time, flailed his arms in the air. "A decision must be made. We have not had luck yet. We cannot lose this trail!" He looked pointedly at the twins. "Are you certain?"

"We're going," said Charlie.

Eve was clearly torn. Ben nodded, but said nothing.

Emma stepped up to Dr. Waldo. "Do you have spare rocks for us? The keys, and the bracelets?"

Dr. Waldo made the decision. He called out to the scientist who had brought Eve's bag, "Two more travel packs, quickly! These two are going along." To Charlie and Emma, he said, "I don't have time to explain anything to you. Stick with Eve. *Do not* lose the bracelets or the key. They are filled with energies, energies you will need. Stick with Eve. Don't stray. Don't lose anything or you may not be able to find your way back. Eve will explain the rest. Stay with her." In his turmoil, he repeated himself without seeming to realize he was even speaking.

Apprehensive but eager, Charlie and Emma picked up their backpacks, which they, too, had left by the elevator. The scientist came back with two travel packs. She handed them to Charlie and Emma.

"Be safe, be safe," said Dr. Waldo, mumbling as he helped Emma put on her bracelet. Eve helped Charlie with his. "Eve, you're sure you're ready to do this without your father? You remember how to operate everything in the elevator?" Dr. Waldo asked.

Eve's head moved almost imperceptibly: Yes. "I'm ready," she said quietly. Ben reached out and held her hand.

"All right then," said Dr. Waldo. "Now go, luck be with you, and come back safe, and soon."

The four teens piled into the elevator. The door to the Hub closed and sealed itself shut behind them.

"So," said Charlie, "yeah, so, what exactly are we looking for?"

"Disturbances," said Eve. "Things that seem wrong. We aren't sure, really. We're just sort of hoping we'll know. We're hoping to find Vik before he destroys everything. That's about it. Now hush; I have to concentrate."

Eve was staring at a panel on the side wall, a panel that Emma would have sworn wasn't there before. Had she missed it, or had Eve somehow made it appear? Not wanting to break Eve's concentration, Emma decided to wait and ask later. Eve typed in a bunch of numbers—coordinates?—paused, typed in some more. At the end, she tapped the tip of her finger on the bottom right of the screen.

"Hang on to something," Eve said. "I always get a little lightheaded." She smiled at Ben. He reached over and held her hand again.

Emma grabbed Charlie's hand.

At first, nothing seemed to happen. Then, there was a slight jolt. The lights in the room flickered. A bigger jolt, and a sound resembling that of a boot being sucked out of mud, a sound that Emma felt she could almost feel in her soul. With the hand not already holding Charlie's hand, Emma grabbed her brother's arm to steady herself; then, overcome with dizziness, she sat down on the floor. Charlie joined her. The pull grew stronger, a pressure that seemed to be crushing in on her from the outside while at the same time threatening to turn her inside out. Emma feared she would faint. The lights flickered off for a long moment, then came back on. The air in the elevator smelled of metal and distant smoke and honey.

And then, everything grew still.

Emma swallowed hard to keep her breakfast down, feeling glad she hadn't had more eggs. She picked herself up from the floor and glanced at Ben and Charlie, who looked as pale as she felt.

Eve seemed pleased with herself, and far less disheveled than the rest of the group. "We're here!" she said. "Fingers crossed, as you guys say!" She reached into her pocket and pulled out a ring.

Emma, breathing slowly through her mouth, realized there was yet another stone on Eve's ring. "What does that one do?" she asked, pointing at the rock.

Eve smiled brightly. "You catch on fast," she said. Emma was taken aback. She'd been thinking of Eve as her adversary, her competitor. She realized she had not been particularly welcoming to this young woman, a stranger on her planet, who had no one for company but her father. She felt ashamed.

She smiled back at Eve. Eve handed her the ring. Emma looked at it with a minimum of real interest; just another rock. "Almost blindingly white," she laughed, but then her laugh stopped abruptly. "Wait." Emma reached for her backpack. "I found a rock just like this on the beach by the lighthouse! I'm sure of it!" She dug into the side pocket of her pack. She hadn't tossed the rock away; she knew she'd kept it. Hadn't she? Coming up empty in the first pocket, she reached her fingers deep into another pocket, feeling around for a firm lump. Nothing. She moved on to a third pocket, but the rock wasn't there.

"Maybe I threw it back," she mused, mostly to herself. The rock she'd found on the beach had been so beautiful. She knew she'd kept it, and she was sure she'd never taken it out of this backpack, but it was nowhere to be found. Nothing to be done for it, Emma sighed. She arranged her mouth into a smile and handed the ring back to Eve. "What does that rock do?"

Eve had been watching Emma's search with a concerned look on her face. Following Emma's lead, though, she said nothing further about Emma's actions. "This rock is an energy rock," she said. "It follows energy trails."

Emma gasped as the memory of finding her own rock came back. It *had* been the same kind of rock! She remembered thinking the sun had gotten into her eyes, but she knew she'd seen trails of light following Charlie when she'd held the rock. She knew it! Frustrated, she reached frantically into her pack again. It had to be there. It had to!

But it wasn't.

"How does it work?" asked Charlie, giving his deflated sister a little pat on the foot, then steadying himself on hands and knees before raising himself up from the floor.

"It's hard to describe until you see it," said Eve. "It tracks people's energy. You can 'charge' it to follow a specific person, which we've done with this one, to Vik's energy. Or if you don't, it'll track the energy of the last person you were thinking about. You have to be touching it for it to work. See this ring?" she said, holding it out for them to inspect. She turned it so they could see the inside of the ring, the side that would touch her finger. "See how the band of the ring has a hole cut out, so that the rock can poke through? That's so the rock can touch my finger. A lot easier than having to hold it in my hand all the time. I used to sometimes forget I was holding a rock, in my excitement, and I'd drop it. So Dr. Waldo had one of his staff make this ring for me."

Emma saw Eve blush again slightly. Against her instincts, she felt herself warming to this girl. "I'd probably drop it, too," she said. "For sure I would. Heck, I've lost the one I had. That was a good idea to make it into a ring."

Eve gave Emma a look of thanks, and put on the ring.

"All right, no time like the present!" she said. "Let's go find Vik!"

The door to the other side opened. Emma found herself holding her breath. What would they find? Where would they—

"Wait," she said.

"What the—" said Charlie.

"But this is the lighthouse lobby," said Ben. "The same lighthouse. The Balky Point lighthouse."

"On our Earth," said Charlie.

They all looked at each other, then at Eve, in confusion.

Eve had no answers. She looked dismayed.

They stepped out of the storage room. Eve looked around. Her blush had deepened, crawled down her neck.

"I must have messed up," she said, her eyes starting to glisten.

Emma felt a rush of sympathy for this alien girl she was starting to think of as a friend. She reached out and gave her a hug. "It's okay. It was your first time, right? Just takes practice, I'm sure. Let's go ask Dr. Waldo. He'll get us back on track."

"We're losing time," said Eve. "He'll be so mad."

"He won't be mad," said Emma. She realized she didn't know Dr. Waldo well enough to make that statement, but it would do no good to get Eve more upset. With an arm around Eve, she led the distraught girl back into the elevator. The young men followed.

Once the door closed behind them, they all waited awkwardly for Eve to open the door to the Hub.

"So, do you need us to help with something?" asked Charlie, poking at the wall to see if there might be a button somewhere.

"Should I try my key?" asked Ben, fishing the wishing rock pendant out from under his shirt again.

Charlie waved his arms around. "Where are the security cameras? Maybe they can see us? Hello! Hello! Open the door please, Dr. Waldo! Hello?" But the door remained stubbornly closed.

"I don't understand," said Eve. "It should be opening. Did I break it? Or did ... oh my gosh. Oh no."

"What?" said Emma, growing alarmed. "Oh my gosh what?"

Eve was shuddering, shaking her head. "Did Vik succeed? Did he unravel this spot? Are my father and I stuck here?" She looked at the others. "I mean no offense. Yours is a beautiful planet. It's just ..." She didn't finish.

Emma put an arm around Eve again. "It's okay. We'll go back

to the cabin, and wait for your father to come back with Ed. He'll know what to do. I'm sure it's just a glitch. When that woman in the Hub told us they'd had a quake while we were off looking at the Experimental Building, it must have jolted something in the elevator. But I'm sure Dr. Waldo will have figured it out, and will be working on it from his side. And your father, fathers always know what to do. Let's just go find him."

Eve listened to Emma's speech with a glazed, grim look on her face. She nodded her consent.

Emma and Charlie looked for their bikes in the shrub by the side of the lighthouse, but someone had taken them. ("Seriously? Seriously?" Charlie said, in disgust.) Ben's brother had dropped him off at the lighthouse, so he didn't have transportation, either.

"As if things weren't bad enough," said Charlie.

The group headed off on the long walk back to the cabin.

"Mom and Dad are going to be so mad that we went off to explore the universes without telling them," Charlie said to Emma as they walked.

"We could just not tell them," suggested Emma. "They don't really need to know, do they?"

A smile broke out across Charlie's face. "Now you're starting to think like me, big sister! Proud of you, Em." He winked his approval at her.

Emma warmed at his happiness and felt a little better. She hadn't even been all that excited about exploring the universes (truth be told, she'd been a lot scared at the prospect), but she had been looking forward to the adventure of it. Assuming they didn't run into any alien dinosaurs or any species whose primary mission in life was to kill humans on sight, or anything of that sort. Gallivanting about the universes was, without a doubt, an unlikely impossibility—which made the possibility of doing it all the more attractive. Emma was not a huge risk taker, but she liked to imagine that she could be one day, if the situation were right and most danger had been removed from the equation. Charlie was far more the type to forge forth without thought for safety or consequence. She admired that in her twin: his ability to throw caution to the wind, his lack of concern for protocol and precedence.

"Aliens aliens aliens," Charlie muttered to himself, in time with his steps, first on every step, then in time with the step of his left foot, then in time with his right. When he grew tired of this, he called out to Eve, who was walking alongside Ben, behind Charlie and Emma. "Hey, Eve. Question. Shouldn't it be something other than 'universes'? Is 'universes' really the plural of 'universe'?" Charlie turned to walk backward, to face Eve and Ben as he spoke, checking over his shoulder frequently to make sure he didn't trip over anything. "I mean, isn't 'universe' meant to imply that there's only one? Like Ben was saying the other night, isn't that what the 'uni' means? Like, a unicycle, it's a bicycle with one wheel. Unicorn, a horse with one horn. Which, obviously, begs the question of why it's a unicorn rather than a unihorn, but either way, it only has one horn. Or one corn, I guess. If there's more than one universe, then doesn't that mean it's not actually a *uni*verse after all?"

Eve laughed. "Charlie, it's English. It's your language, not mine. But we often say 'multiverse.'"

Reaching out to guide backward-walking Charlie around a large pothole, Emma pondered the question. "Yes, 'uni' means one, but that doesn't mean you can't have more than one universe. There's more than one unicycle in the world. There are unicycles, plural. If unicorns existed, there could be more than one. I think you can call it a 'universe' and still have more than one. If you wanted to refer to all the universes together as one unit, then maybe you'd say 'polyverse' or, like Eve said, 'multiverse.' But I'm in favor of 'universes' for a plural. I don't think there's anything wrong with that." She looked at Ben to see what he thought.

"I agree," he said. "Universes makes sense to me. Just like unicorns and unicycles."

"Unicorns do exist, you know" said Eve, with an air of casual revelation.

Charlie pumped his right arm in the air in a gesture of triumph. "Yes! Unicorns exist? Really? Where?"

"We saw them once, I can't remember where. Sometimes, we are somewhere but we aren't really sure where that somewhere is. Anyway, we saw them once. I don't know if these were flying unicorns, but they were definitely very much like what you people think of as unicorns."

Charlie turned to Emma. "You realize, of course, that the rhinoceros is basically a portly unicorn without fur, right?" He looked mighty pleased with himself, and started walking facing forward again. Emma just shook her head in response.

Changing the subject, Emma took the opportunity to talk with the gentleman she'd been too shy to say much to yet. "Ben, what did your parents say when you told them you were going to go explore the universes? Did they say it was a bad idea? Or were they all in?"

Ben didn't speak immediately. "They were okay with it, I guess," he said, finally.

"Did you tell them?" asked Charlie.

"I may not have told them everything," he admitted, clearing his throat and kicking a stick off to the side of the road. "I told them what they needed to know."

Something about this was a relief to Emma. She'd been putting Ben so high above all the rest of them. To know he might have fudged a bit in talking with his parents, too, was reassuring somehow.

"Do they even know you've been cavorting with aliens?" Emma asked.

Ben gave her a sheepish smile. "They know. Ed came over and told them everything. That man, he likes a good story. He had to tell Dad that the whole UFO thing was real. They were up half the night two nights ago, taking ten minutes worth of information and making it last for hours. So, yes, they know that part. Ed didn't tell them I wanted to go along. He left that for me. He did tell them he was going to look around with Milo, though. They told him to be careful. I figured if looking around the island made them worried, then maybe they couldn't handle my going off to explore the polyverse."

Emma's heart fluttered, just a bit, on hearing him use her word.

"I may have told them I was going camping for a couple days," Ben confessed. "My brother knows the truth, though. If something had happened and I hadn't come back, he'd have known. It's not like I left without telling anyone. In fact," he said, looking around at the all-too-familiar island, "it's not like I left, at all."

"I hear you bro," said Charlie, giving voice and solidarity to his own dejection. "Dead elevator: 1; Charlie: 0."

Eve looked sad, and Emma realized she might be taking all this too much to heart. "It's not your fault, Eve," she said. "Don't listen to them. They were just excited about going off on some cowboy adventure, but they probably couldn't have handled it, anyway. It's not your fault. And the elevator isn't dead." She shot a disapproving look at Charlie. "It's just not working right now. You'll get home. Don't worry. We'll make sure you get home."

Each lost in his or her own thoughts, eventually the foursome reached the cabin. When they got there, they saw a strange car in the driveway.

"Whose car is that?" asked Charlie. "Ben, do you recognize it? Our car is gone, too. I wonder if Mom or Dad went to join Milo and Ed?" he said. A bitter note in his voice indicated his disappointment in the abrupt end of his own exploits.

The front door was open. Emma walked in first, followed by Charlie and the others. "Mom! Dad! We're back!" she called out with forced cheerfulness.

Amy Renee came rushing out from the kitchen with a look of horror on her face.

Emma was immediately alarmed. "Mom, what is it? Is Dad okay? Ed and Milo? What's wrong?"

The look on her own face, however, quickly turned to horror as well.

Behind Amy Renee, coming out of the kitchen, was Charlie. Another Charlie. And then, behind him, another Emma.

"Oh, no, oh, no, oh no …" said Eve. She turned to Emma, at her side, and said in a low voice, "Emma, I think I've really messed up … I don't think this is your Earth."

Emma, Charlie, Eve, and Ben were sitting in the cabin's living room with the other Emma (whom Charlie had dubbed "Parallel Emma"), the other Charlie ("Parallel Charlie"), Amy Renee ("Parallel Mom"), and Glen ("Parallel Dad"). On this Earth, the Nelsons had never heard of Milo or Eve. They knew Ed, and this was indeed his cabin, but he wasn't there at the time. They knew nothing about the lighthouse or all the universes it held within its walls. Eve, who had realized what this meant for her own situation—she had no idea where her father was, where she was, or how to get to Dr. Waldo—explained the situation as calmly as she could.

Both Earthlings and parallel Earthlings were in a bit of shock.

"Another Earth. You're saying there's another *Earth*. If the two of you weren't here," said Parallel Amy Renee, indicating Emma and Charlie, "I don't know that I'd believe you. You say you got here in … an *elevator?*" The disbelief in her voice was clear.

Emma knew that tone well. If it hadn't happened to her, she wouldn't have believed it either. "Not an elevator, really. That's just what they call it. It's … well, it's a portal, or a doorway."

"Does it move? I don't understand how it works. Is it a spaceship?" asked Glen, literally sitting on the edge of his seat, leaning forward, as though being closer to the strange visitors might somehow help him understand the impossible things they were saying.

"It, uh …" Emma looked at Eve for help.

"To be honest, I'm not entirely sure what happens," said Eve. "Obviously, we can't stand outside and watch. The room seals itself up. It certainly feels like it's moving, but I guess I don't actually know if it does. And I don't know what would happen if someone else tried to use it at the same time we were using it. Sort of like an elevator, we think there's just one portal for anyone to use at any one time. But it's not a spaceship, no. It can't go just anywhere. It's fixed, in a way. Fixed in one spot in the universes." She gave them the tied-quilt analogy her father had used when explaining to Emma, Charlie, and Ben. "There are millions of others, throughout the planets and universes, but each of them just works within a fixed point. At least, as far as we know."

On hearing herself use the phrase Charlie had accused Dr. Waldo of overusing, Eve smiled softly and her eyes twinkled. She looked at Charlie and tossed him a knowing laugh. "As far as we know," she repeated.

Charlie caught her laugh and returned it twofold.

Parallel Charlie, as yet unfettered with undying love for Eve, wanted to hear more about the other Earth. He wanted to know everything. "Exactly how much of your Earth and our Earth is alike, and how much is different?" he asked, as though anyone there were qualified to answer. "We're twins, you're twins. This island is Dogwinkle Island here and where you're from. But the car we rented is different from the car you rented." In the course of discussion, they'd learned the car out front, which Charlie had surmised must belong to someone else, was actually this parallel family's rental car. "So there are small differences. Are there big differences? Are you guys from Minsota too?"

Emma and Charlie looked at each other. "You mean Minnesota?" said Emma.

"Minsota," said Parallel Charlie, shaking his head. "Our original home state, before we moved out west, was Minsota."

"Minnesota: Canada to the north, North and South Dakota to the west, Iowa to the south, Wisconsin to the east?" asked Emma.

"Minsota: Canada to the north, Dakota to the west, Iowa to the south, Wisconsin to the east," said Parallel Charlie.

"No. Minnesota. But your planet, it's called Earth, right? That's the same?" asked Charlie.

"Earth. Indeed," said Parallel Charlie.

"Eight planets in the solar system?" said Charlie.

"No, nine. Huh." Parallel Charlie gave an exaggerated frown.

"Did you guys get to keep Pluto?" asked Charlie. "We totally had to give up Pluto. Poor Pluto."

"No, there's no Pluto," said Parallel Emma. "Our planets are Hermes, Aphrodite, Earth, Ares, Zeus, Kronos, Hera, Poseidon, Dis."

Emma's eyes lit up with recognition. "Named after the Greek gods rather than the Roman gods!" she said, quite pleased with herself. "Ours are the same. Just different names for them. The Roman god Mercury is the Greek god Hermes; the Roman goddess Venus is the Greek goddess Aphrodite; and so on. Our planets are Mercury, Venus, Earth, Mars, Jupiter, Saturn, Uranus, Neptune.

Dis would be Pluto, god of wealth. Uranus isn't Hera, though, but I guess I'd rather have a planet Hera than a planet Uranus, frankly." She wrinkled her nose in disfavor. "That's weird, actually. Uranus is a Greek god. It would have been nice if they'd named the planet Caelus, after the Roman god, like all the other planets. Caelus is the Roman version of Uranus, 'Father Sky.' But no, they bucked the trend to go with with Uranus. Bad move, planet namers." Two years prior, Emma had had to do a science report on Uranus, and her classmates never let her forget it. She was still annoyed with 18th century German astronomer Johann Elert Bode for even suggesting the planet name.

"Same gods, different names. That's crazy," said Charlie. He fist-bumped Parallel Charlie. "Awesome."

Emma had pulled out her notebook and was making a list of all the differences between Earth and this parallel Earth.

"What's the list for?" asked Ben.

Emma blushed. "I just … I make lists. I like order, I guess. And lists."

"She makes a lot of lists," said Charlie.

"Me too," smiled Parallel Emma, reaching to give an awkward fist bump to her parallel self. Emma smiled back at her alter self, and added that bit of information to her list.

"Sorry, guys, I know this is fascinating—unbelievable but fascinating—and I'd love to learn more, too, but this isn't helping us, and it's not helping Eve get back to her father," said Parallel Amy Renee. She turned to Eve. "What do you propose we do, Eve? I'm sorry, but this is beyond my ken. How can we help you?"

For a moment, Eve looked frightened at the responsibility. Then, she closed her eyes and took a deep breath, willing away the fear. "Okay. Okay. We need to see if we can get back into the Hub yet. If we can't, then we need to look around here. I thought we'd come to the wrong place—I thought we were still on the other Earth—but maybe this *is* where Dr. Waldo meant us to go. Maybe Vik is here, after all. We need to look around for him." She shook her head. "It took us forever to walk here from the lighthouse. We probably lost him already. I should have been paying attention." She twirled the ring on her finger, the one with the rock that, through the back of the band, was in constant contact with her skin. "I wasn't paying attention. I thought we hadn't gone anywhere so I didn't even look. But we need to try to find Vik here. We can't give up just yet." Finally, she landed on a plan of action that satisfied her, and her mood calmed. "We'll look for Vik first. Then, whether we find him or not, we'll figure out a way to get back into the Hub."

Despite being somewhat confused about the whole parallel Earth scenario, the parallel family quickly rallied around Eve's plan. In the end, due simply to the size of their rental car, it was decided that Parallel Charlie and Parallel Emma would join Charlie, Emma, Eve, and Ben on the quest to find Vik, and the parents would stay home. Ben wanted to go find Parallel Ben, but Eve convinced him there was no time for that.

"Can we come back one day and meet him?" Ben asked. How often would any of them have a chance to meet a true doppelgänger?

"I'm not even sure how we got here in the first place," Eve said. As it wasn't a flat-out "no," Ben held out hope and agreed to move on with the search.

The six teens piled into the car. Parallel Charlie drove; Eve sat next to him in the middle front seat, but she was practically in Ben's lap, in the passenger seat. Charlie sat in the middle in the back, with Parallel Emma on his left, and Emma on his right.

"Not exactly the seating configuration I would have chosen," said Charlie, eyeing with jealousy how close Eve was to Ben. From either side of him, both Parallel Emma and Emma punched Charlie in the arm. "Definitely not how I would have arranged us," he mumbled.

They drove around the island a while, none of them quite sure what they were looking for. Eve held the energy-tracing rock in her hand, checking it constantly to see if it was giving off any signals. It was not.

"What do we do if we find this guy?" asked Parallel Charlie. "I'd say between the six of us we can hold him, but is there a Multiverse Police we can call to come get him?" In the course of driving around, Eve, Ben, Emma, and Charlie had pretty much gotten Parallel Charlie and Parallel Emma up to speed on the idea of the multiverse.

"Multiverse Police," repeated Charlie, snickering. "We are funny, funny people, Parallel Charlie. To think there are two of us. The universes are so lucky!" He and Parallel Charlie high-fived.

"No Multiverse Police," said Eve. "Dad and I each have a device to use if we find him, it'll send him straight back to our planet—and universe, obviously—where they'll deal with him. At least, that's the idea. Testing was … well, it wasn't entirely consistent. But it's the best we have. Dr. Waldo calls them 'pigeons,' named after the idea of homing pigeons. They can't take you everywhere, but they can be calibrated to take you to one specific place—in our case, home."

Eve's words sounded ominous. "What do you mean, 'testing wasn't consistent'?" asked Emma, suppressing an urge to ask to see the pigeon. She didn't want to look overeager.

"Well," said Eve, "There may have been occasions on which the object that was supposed to be sent home, actually was … sort of obliterated."

"Obliterated?" asked Parallel Charlie, swerving slightly on the road. "Obliterated how?"

"We think the particles of the object were … spread out, more or less. That's our best guess, based on the particles that did come through. But," she said with forced cheerfulness, "that was in early tests. Almost all the later testing went perfectly well."

"'Almost all,'" said Emma. "Remind me not to use one of those 'pigeons.'" Traveling the universes sounded fun, she thought, but only so long as she actually remained in one piece.

"Dr. Waldo didn't tell me all that," said Ben, his eyes wide.

"What do you mean? When did you talk with him about the pigeons?" asked Eve.

"When I first came back to the Hub, by myself. He and I talked a while about my coming along with you. He gave me a pigeon, too, in case we find Vik. But he didn't say it could obliterate anyone." He looked sobered and a little distressed. What other critical information had Dr. Waldo withheld?

"Well, it's not meant for any of us to use, anyway," said Eve. "And Dr. Waldo has always been an optimist. He's probably assuming he's got all the bugs worked out. And maybe he has. He tinkers with these all the time, takes back the ones we have and gives us new ones that he says will work better. If he gave you one, it's probably even more accurate than mine. Don't worry. You won't need to use it anyway. We'll use mine instead."

Despite her words, Ben did not look reassured.

Charlie, however, was agitated to learn that yet again, Ben had won the Multiverse Lottery. First, Ben got to come along without playing tricks on his parents. Second, he got to sit with—or practically under—Eve in this car. And now this. Emma could feel Charlie's aggravation emanating from him. Even Parallel Emma knew something was bothering her parallel twin, but she didn't have enough information to know what it was. Emma and Parallel Emma exchanged a look of commiseration. He may be an idiot, but he was their idiot, and it didn't make them happy to see him distressed.

After driving around aimlessly for two hours and finding absolutely nothing, Eve declared the mission a failure and said the best thing to do would be for the non-parallels to go back to the Hub and try to get back in. "Maybe whatever was wrong has been fixed," she said, though she didn't sound hopeful.

They drove back to the cabin to say goodbye to Parallel Amy Renee and Parallel Glen, and then Parallel Charlie drove all the teens to the lighthouse.

"Can we come in?" Parallel Charlie asked. "To the elevator? Just to see?"

But Eve was adamant. They'd already wasted enough time. They needed to get back to the Hub, get back to the search.

That is, if Eve could get them back at all.

chapter eight

Walking through the lighthouse lobby that looked exactly like the one on their own Earth, the travelers piled into the storage room. "At least that worked," said Eve. For whatever reason, the wishing rock master key would still unlock the door from the lobby into the elevator. But when Eve tried to get through to the Hub again, the inside door remained stubbornly closed.

"No!" cried out Eve in frustration. "No, no, no!" She pounded her fists on the wall that stood between her and the safety of the Hub and let out a primal scream. "Let us in! Dr. Waldo, let us in!" Ben reached out for her, and the young woman collapsed into his arms.

Whether or not Dr. Waldo heard them, the door remained closed.

Emma felt Eve's pain. Eve was separated from her father and her world, as now Emma and Charlie and Ben were separated from their own Earth. Emma felt certain that if they were stuck here, all the parallel families would take them in, but it wouldn't be the same. And what of their own parents and families, back home? She and Charlie had run off without saying a thing, sneaking away, certain that they'd go off, discover new planets, find Vik, and be home before dinner. Now what? Everything had gone wrong. She had no idea what to do. She was glad Eve had sent Parallel Charlie and Parallel Emma home. They were nice enough, obviously, but coping with the reality of their existence on top of everything else would have been just too much at the moment. She turned to her brother and slouched into his shoulder for comfort. He wrapped his arms around her and placed his chin on top of her head.

Eve rested in Ben's embrace, deep in thought, staring at the wall. In a moment, however, her demeanor changed from despair to resolve. She stood up straight with a look of firm determination. "I'm getting you guys home," she said. "I just am." Without stopping to warn the others to hang on to something, Eve punched coordinates into the panel. She braced herself against the wall, and they waited.

At first, nothing. Then, the sound of the boot being sucked out of the mud. The dizziness. The insides turning out. The metallic smoky honey smell.

The silence.

The corners of Eve's mouth turned up in a weak smile. "We're home?"

She opened the door to the outside.

Looking over Eve's shoulder, Ben shook his head slowly. "I don't think this is home," he said.

Through the open door, a roar of surging water crashed all around them and echoed throughout the interior of the traveling storage room. Holding tight to the frame of the door with one hand and reaching behind her to hold on to Charlie with the other, Emma peered cautiously around the door frame. Spray from a crashing wave spattered her face, and she ducked immediately back into the safety of the elevator. "What in the world!" she said, wiping her face with her sleeve. She looked out again.

This elevator was definitely not tucked serenely inside a quiet lighthouse like those on Earth. On this world, this elevator was perched quite precariously on a jagged island, a tiny bit of barren lava-like reef jutting out above the roiling waters of an endless sea. The drop-off from the elevator to the water was only a few feet beyond the open door. There was not another bit of land in sight. The ocean churned around them, threatening sinisterly to reach in with a fickle wave and grab the youngsters, forever claiming them for the watery depths of this planet.

"Not here!" said Eve. She closed the door rapidly, just as a great swell of water burst against the rock they'd landed on.

With the door shut on the wet world, the cacophony of the sea disappeared. The only sound was that of the four teens, breathing hard.

Emma's heart was beating as fast as one of Dr. Waldo's jigs. "What was that?" she said, catching her breath.

Eve shook her head. "Wrong planet, that's for sure. No way Vik could be there," she said. She looked at the panel. "Try again, Eve, try again," she muttered to herself.

Still unsettled, the others watched without word as Eve input more coordinates into the device on the elevator wall. Eve grasped at the wishing rock pendant around her neck as she finished the sequence.

"Here goes nothing again," she said.

Boot sucking. Wooziness. Smoke.

The door opened.

In complete contrast to the watery world they'd just escaped, this planet spread out before them arid and thirsty as far as the eye could see in the blazing light. Not one bush, tree, or hill marred the horizon. An occasional gust of wind lifted the dust in a stunted short-lived swirl.

Emma's throat felt parched just looking at the scene.

Taking off her jacket as the torrid heat crowded out the cool air within the elevator, Eve stepped cautiously outside. The others followed. Ben set down his own jacket just outside the elevator door.

"So we can find the door again," he said at Emma's inquiring look.

Emma didn't understand, but didn't want to admit her ignorance. She just nodded.

The group wandered slowly and aimlessly away from the safety of the elevator. Looking for what, no one could say; the terrain harbored no secrets, unless they were underground. A flat nothingness surrounded them. Emma spun slowly in a circle to survey all the land. She saw nothing.

Nothing! She suddenly panicked. Where was the elevator? She could see the lump of Ben's jacket, but nothing else.

"Eve!" she said. "The elevator! It's gone!"

Eve turned back toward where they'd come from, and saw the nothingness where there once had been something, but her expression didn't change. "It's okay," she said. "That's what happens. There's no building here to hide the elevator, so it hides itself. But it's still there. You have your necklace on, right, with the wishing rock?"

Emma nodded.

"So, if you go closer, you'll sort of 'feel' the elevator again. Think about the elevator and let the universes know you want in, and when you're close enough, the door will open. Don't worry," she continued with a smile. "You get used to it. This isn't my first rodeo, as you all say."

Emma looked at Ben, who was grinning from ear to ear. Clearly, he'd already been told about this disappearing act. His black jacket stood out darkly on the beige landscape, an inky bread crumb to help them find their way back.

To convince herself that they were all still safe, Emma did as Eve said—she walked closer to Ben's jacket. Just as Eve had promised, after a few steps Emma started to feel a vibration. It didn't seem to be coming from the wishing rock on the cord around her neck, but rather from all around her. Her skin hummed, her ears filled with a silent thrumming. "Yes," she said. "Even without the jacket I'd know. We're close. I can tell." Not quite sure how to talk to the universes, she sent out a hesitant thought: *Open the door, please? Universes, please open the door?* With another step she was close enough, and the door slid open.

"Definitely smart," Emma said to Ben, nodding at his jacket.

Emma moved away from the elevator and the door closed again. The elevator disappeared.

One hand on his hip, another shielding his eyes from the glaring sunlight, Charlie surveyed the unchanging landscape. "He can't be here, can he?" he asked Eve. "Where could he even go?"

Holding her right hand out in front of her, the hand with the energy rock ring calibrated to Vik's energy, Eve squinted and blinked. "We don't know what else is out there. It looks like a whole lot of nothing from here, but there could be a city just over the horizon. Still, to get there he'd have to walk there, and that's a long way to go. I agree, I don't think he's here. It's just—" Eve shook her right hand. "I can't tell—the light is tricky." She looked up into the sky. "Two suns, that doesn't help. I don't think I'm seeing energy trails, but the light, it's making mirages or something in the air, it's so hard to tell." She shook her head, then involuntarily shuddered. "This place is awful. Gives me the creeps. Nothing could live here," she said. "I'm not even sure we could."

"Wait!" said Charlie. "Can we breathe? Is there oxygen?" He inhaled deeply several times, as if breathing more would answer his question.

"We're fine," said Emma. "Remember, the bracelets? The amber with the air bubble? Remember what Dr. Waldo said, the atmospheric shield?" She reached out for his left arm, where the bracelet was securely clasped around his wrist. "You're fine, Charles," she said. "Pay attention. Calm down."

Eve pointed at her bracelet. "Probably using the air bubble right now," she agreed.

Emma inhaled deeply, grateful for the amber rock that provided them with the oxygen they were used to. Her exhale was almost a sigh as she scanned this foreign planet. Nothing here but nothing, she thought, but yet felt compelled to explore, at least a little bit. Who knew when she'd have another opportunity like this? The absence of anything but dust and sun felt bleak, but at the same time there was a peaceful calm in the lack. No encumbrances. No material goods to have or not have and be judged against. No confusing people to baffle and frustrate her. She walked slowly in the direction of one of the suns, mesmerized by the void around her.

Hearing Eve's twinkling laughter, Emma looked back. She'd wandered farther than she realized. Eve, Ben, and Charlie were laughing, sharing a joke she wasn't a part of. Like always. Even here, millions or billions or who knew how many miles away from home.

I could just stay here and they wouldn't even notice.

The words appeared fully formed in Emma's head without her bidding, but as she thought them she knew it was true.

She looked at the bracelet on her wrist. *I'm sure I can breathe without this,* she thought. *The air is just fine here.* Something in her told her it was true. She reached to take it off.

"Em! What are you doing!" The others had decided there was no point in staying, and Charlie had jogged over to get his sister, just as she'd released the bracelet's hidden clasp. "Put that back on!" He reached out, grabbed her hand and the bracelet, and snapped it back on her wrist.

"What were you thinking, Emma Ree?" Charlie studied her eyes, his face contorted with worry.

She stared at him. What indeed had she been thinking?

Catching her hand in his, Charlie led Emma back toward Eve and Ben, who were standing by Ben's jacket at the open elevator door. Emma felt dazed, puzzled by her own actions. *What happened back there?* Seeking to comfort herself, Emma reached out and punched Charlie on the shoulder. "Dork," she said softly.

But Charlie didn't return the punch like he usually did. Instead, he gave her a wide smile, then let go of her hand and ran off ahead to join the others.

Once they were all in the elevator with the door sealed shut behind them, Emma's head seemed to clear a bit. *That was weird,* she thought. *The epitome of discombobulating.* Maybe she wasn't quite as ready to travel the universes as she'd thought.

Eve, determined to get them back to Dr. Waldo, stood and stared at the wall that should have let them back into the Hub. If sheer force of gaze could have opened it, she would have opened it with her eyes. But the entrance remained resolutely closed.

Defeated, she turned once again to the operations panel. "I know I have the right numbers. I know I do," she said.

"Could you have reversed something?" Emma suggested gently. She felt helpless and lost, in more ways than one. Sensing Eve felt the same thing was not a comfort.

Eve leaned her forehead against the wall and let out a string of English curse words under her breath. *So she's learned the more colorful parts of our language, too,* Emma thought. She reached out and soothed Eve's glorious silver-blonde hair. "It'll be okay," she said. But would it?

"Try again," Eve scolded herself, raising her head. She looked at the panel and whispered numbers out loud as she tapped them in.

With a final "... seven, nine," she hit the "enter" button.

Fearing she might fall over from fatigue and an existential weariness, Emma sat down on the floor to wait out the dizziness and the other sensations that were now becoming all too familiar. She forced herself to take long, slow, deep breaths as the universes spun and whirled her from one unknown spot to another. *If the universes will listen when I want a door opened,* she thought, *maybe they'll listen to other messages.* She sent up a wish to any forces that might be willing to hear: *Please, let us go home.*

The room settled again. The teens looked at each other with anxiety and hope. The door to the outside slid open. A warm, gentle breeze blew in.

Once again, definitely not home.

Every sense on alert, the foursome walked slowly and quietly out of the security of the storage closet into a bright night on another alien world. The dim light indicated evening or nighttime, but two moons, high in the sky, lit the landscape and created long, eerie shadows. One moon seemed about four times the size of Earth's moon; the second, near the first but slightly lower in the sky, appeared to be much smaller. Whether waxing or waning, it wasn't clear, but both were nearly full. The air smelled like freshly watered house plants, Emma thought, a smell of damp earth. Was it earth if it wasn't Earth? *Damp dirt, then,* Emma corrected herself in her mind. A scent that indicated there may have been a recent rain. The sky was more or less cloud-free, but that meant nothing.

The shadows seemed to move, to play tricks on the eye. Was that a creature moving over there, or just the low leaves of a tree, rustling in the wind? "Shhhh," said Emma, to no one in particular.

"Why are we being quiet?" Charlie replied in a loud whisper, crouching beside his sister. He breathed in and out forcefully, testing the air, or testing the amber rock on his bracelet.

"Because we do not know one darned thing about this place. Look around. This place is absolutely ripe for dinosaurs," said Emma. "Be quiet or a velociraptor will come swipe you."

There were no velociraptors nor any other kind of dinosaurs in sight, but the land did have the look and feel of an ancient Earth. Some plants had leaves the size of umbrellas or larger. Others plants resembled giant palm trees. Everything was massive, in fact. Emma felt as if she'd been shrunk into Alice in Wonderland's world.

Ben, however, was enchanted. "Maybe it's more of a Utopia than a Jurassic Park," he suggested. "I mean, smell that."

Normally when someone told her to "smell that," Emma did not comply—especially if that someone was Charlie—but for Ben, she did. She inhaled deeply and her nose was rewarded with a mingling of lush floral and tropical scents. She couldn't see the source of the smells, but her instincts told her it was a combination of flowers, fruits, and other unknown unearthly wonders.

"Delicious," she said as she exhaled. "Intoxicating. I wish there were more light so we could see." She looked up at the sky and realized there were not two, but three moons. A third was just coming up over the horizon, whereas the two they'd first seen were quickly rising higher in the sky, illuminating the planet below. "Three moons!" she said. "A person could write a nice romantic love song with three moons." In the darkness, she blushed.

"Can we stay a while?" asked Charlie. "I mean, we just got here, and it's our first real alien planet. Other than the other Earth, of course, which was so much like our Earth that it didn't count. And the water planet. And the dead planet. This is the first *interesting* one. Can we look around?"

Emma had a feeling Eve would say no, though she, too, hoped for a "yes." Just long enough for the sun to come up—or maybe suns again?—so they could see the landscape in the daytime. Long enough to explore the trees and maybe find a river or lake to sit by. Even in the darkness, this planet seemed beautiful.

Sure enough, Eve was eager to move on. "We can only stay for a minute or two. We have to get back," she said. "I don't know how, but we have to get back to the Hub. We have to find Dr. Waldo, and we have to find my dad."

Emma noticed that Eve hadn't mentioned Vik. Priorities had changed, at this point. Milo came first. Vik could come later.

The group had wandered a good ways from the elevator again, but this time Ben had not left his jacket behind; it would have just been lost in the night.

"Make note of where the elevator is, everyone," said Eve. "Look around for landmarks, recognizable groupings of trees, anything that will help us find our way back."

Charlie looked in the direction they'd come from. "It's invisible again! Let me try that vibration thing—" he said, about to run back to where he thought the elevator was hiding. He stopped abruptly as Ben held out one arm, as though to keep a passenger in a car from flying through the windshield when stopping suddenly.

"What is it?" said Eve in a whisper so low it was barely audible.

Ben's breathing was shallow. Moving as little as possible, he pointed at an area just left of where the elevator had been.

"I don't—" Emma said, but then, she saw it too.

Eyes. The unmistakable glow of eyes, almost hidden within the giant foliage.

A cloud shifted off the largest moon, and the landscape grew brighter. Shadows shifted, and the creatures that owned the eyes emerged ever so slightly from the darkness.

These were the eyes of people, intelligent beings.

People with spears.

People with spears, pointed at them.

The people with spears bolted forward.

"RUN!" Eve cried out. Grabbing Emma by the hand, she pulled her along at top speed. Ben and Charlie raced behind them. They tracked through the unfamiliar terrain, tripping on roots and rocks and thorns, scratching and tearing their way through the dense foliage without looking back to see if they were even still being chased. Eve somehow managed to keep hold of Emma's hand, and changed direction to run toward a hill. With nothing else to do but trust Eve, Emma followed.

They'd been running for several minutes when Eve, still dragging Emma, nimbly slipped through a gap between two rocks and pulled Emma in behind her. Panting, she tapped a device on her wrist, and a dim red light illuminated the tiny space they'd found. The crack, which Emma couldn't imagine how Eve had even found, opened up to a larger space inside the hill. Not quite a cave, but more than an indentation in the wall. After determining they were alone in the dark space, they sat down on some large boulders to catch their breaths.

"But aren't we trapped now?" whispered Emma between gasps. It had been a while since she'd run that far and that hard. "They can get us in here. We're as good as dead."

Eve looked at her and shook her head in a gesture of helplessness. "I didn't know what else to do. I kept tripping. I was scared we'd fall and hurt ourselves and die out there, from exposure or worse. I saw this crack in the rock, and just hoped—" She didn't finish her sentence.

"Wait, where are Charlie and Ben?" Emma dashed to the opening they'd slipped through and peered out into the shadows. She saw nothing, just the movement of leaves in the soft warm wind, but no Charlie, no Ben. No natives, either, which was good, but she kept squinting, trying to see some sign of her brother or their friend so she could wave them down and hasten them over to join her and Eve in the tight space. While running, they hadn't had time or opportunity or foresight to make sure everyone stayed together, and now Charlie and Ben were nowhere to be seen. Had they been speared by the natives? Were they still alive? The fear, the thought of what was and could be happening, the running, all of it made her want to throw up or cry.

She chose crying.

Eve moved from her boulder to sit with Emma on hers. With one arm she cradled Emma against her, shushed her and comforted her without words.

When Emma calmed down a bit, Eve moved back to her own boulder.

"I'm sure they're okay," Eve said.

"You don't know that," said Emma.

"I don't know that," Eve said, "but we may as well assume the best. Worrying will get us nowhere."

Emma couldn't argue, but neither could she help herself. *Calm down,* she told herself. *Calm down so you can think.*

She wiped the tears from her eyes. Now she understood how Eve and Milo might have gotten a little disheveled, the night they showed up at the cabin. It seemed so long ago. How long ago was it? Who could really say? Did her parents even know yet that she and Charlie were gone? Where were they in time, anyway? Too many questions, none of which could be answered. She looked at Eve, the shadow of Eve in the darkness. "So now what?" she said.

Eve shrugged. "I guess we wait a bit. Maybe it'll be daytime soon." She poked at buttons on the device on her wrist again. "Looks like the night here is sixteen hours. We've got about four hours left before the sun comes up." In the dim red glow she saw Emma's look of surprise. "One of Dr. Waldo's inventions," she said. "It's not all magic rocks, you know. Technology is pretty awesome, too." She looked back to study the device. "Three moons are up, another should come up soon, and then the sun. Just one sun."

"That's quite an app," said Emma.

"Dr. Waldo loves creating these things," Eve laughed. "Thank goodness you guys finally got cell phones. When we first got to Earth we had to hide all our gadgets so no one would get suspicious. I had to carry this in my pocket," she said, indicating the device on her wrist, "and I was always scared I'd lose it. Now, it just blends in. People might be curious but they aren't suspicious."

Emma gave a grunt of agreement. A sudden wave of exhaustion washed over. She couldn't remember ever being so tired, tired to her very core. Resigned to a few long hours in the tight space, Emma tried to get comfortable on the boulder. She leaned against the wall and found a position where a minimum of bumps were poking into her back. She could only imagine what it would be like to show up on Earth a hundred years ago, knowing what she knew now in the modern day. It would be hard, she thought, not to somehow slip up and reveal something that wasn't meant to be known yet. It might also be hard to resist temptation to change the future, or the past, however one looked at it. Buy a winning lottery ticket, prevent a war, get in the path of someone else's love life for the benefit of one's own.

She looked at the alien girl across from her. What a strange thing, she thought, what an unimaginable thing. Sitting in a cave on some foreign planet—who knew where in the multiverse—talking with a girl about her same age, from another world. Who would have ever imagined? Who would even believe it? And yet, somehow, it seemed despite the impossibilities, they shared common ground.

"Do you like it?" Emma asked, carefully tipping her head against the rough wall. "Traveling like this? Is it fun?"

Eve didn't speak immediately. She looked at the device on her wrist, ran her fingers over the rock-filled bracelet.

"It's what I do, I guess. Dad's all I have, and this is what he's doing. And it's important." She looked Emma in the eye. "Very important."

Emma was thrown off by Eve's intensity, but decided now was the time to get some answers. "You all have never really told us what's up with this Vik dude," she said.

"No, I suppose we haven't," said Eve.

"Well, I've got time now," said Emma, shifting against the bruising rocks. "What's the story?"

Eve laughed. "It's a long story. Where do I begin? It's a story that has taken us a long time to piece together." She paused for a minute, organizing her thoughts. "Okay. You know about the elevators. We used to think no one had ever discovered elevators on Napori, but it turns out that's not true."

"Napori?" said Emma. "I don't think you've mentioned that before. What is Napori?"

"Ah," said Eve. "Backing up even more. I can't always remember what we've told you. So, Napori is what we on Lero call our mother planet. Bigger than Lero. It's where our people evolved. All our people used to live there, but it became too crowded, too overpopulated. Our ancestors were using up all the space and all the resources, fast. They had to do something. They knew about Lero, knew it was habitable, and they already had mastered space travel, so the solution was pretty obvious. A couple hundred people left and established a home on Lero. Other people followed after a while. But it's a long journey, and, well, the split was more than just physical. Same galaxy, but not really all that close. Not what you'd call convenient for visiting."

Eve paused, and Emma thought she might not go on. She waited patiently, and was rewarded.

"So, we used to think no one had ever discovered elevators on Napori, as I was saying, but we were wrong. A long time ago on Napori—shortly after people left to populate Lero—someone discovered an elevator," Eve continued. "He accessed the elevator, used it, but didn't know what he was doing, obviously, and in the process he accidentally killed some people. He was so ashamed that he never told anyone, and no one else ever knew about that elevator. But, unbeknownst to that man and to everyone, in discovering the elevator, he'd awakened some dark forces. As it turns out, not telling anyone about it made it worse.

"Then, as you know," Eve went on, "a while later, my great great aunt—Great Aunt Doethine—discovered the first elevator on Lero. When she did, she was so excited that she told everyone, told all the scientific community, and lots of people got involved in studying it. Thus, the Hub, all the scientists. We don't use the elevators all the time, but by opening up the Hub, we've made that elevator an active, dynamic, creative place. That may seem like a trivial point, but it matters. I have come to believe the elevators are meant to be used. We—intelligent life throughout the universes—are meant to connect with each other. We're meant to explore and discover.

"Anyway. Vik, he's from Lero. He used to be just a normal guy on Lero, living a normal, happy Lero life. Then he and his best friend, a guy he'd known his whole life and who was like a brother to him, they visited Napori—they took the space shuttle, traveled the old-fashioned way. Maybe a year ago, one of our years. When they came back, they were changed, different people. Angry, a little mad. Like madness mad. Not all right in the head anymore."

Eve stared at the cave wall, lost in her story. "Something happened on Napori, obviously, but no one knew what. It had to do with that elevator on Napori. They found it and used it, and something went wrong. Vik's friend was more affected at first. ... they've never let all the details out, but Vik's friend eventually died. Vik was devastated, and he started to get even angrier, crazier. Then, Dr. Waldo got wind of it, started putting the pieces together, and he started investigating.

"What he discovered shocked everyone.

"As it turns out, there was an entity ... hard to describe it ... a thing, not really one entity but not really many separate entities, either. Anyway, its existence was somehow tied to that elevator. We don't really know how elevators work, but obviously they somehow fold space and time, maybe work with black holes or wormholes, we don't quite know. But somewhere in all the workings was something Dr. Waldo started calling The Void.

"The Void is probably as old as time. It seems to be able to hibernate indefinitely until it finds a source of nourishment. When people use elevators, they open doors or gateways, provide The Void access to the universe. And when that first man on Napori opened up an elevator, it seems The Void discovered—maybe rediscovered—that it thrives on people's feelings of isolation and loneliness."

"It eats loneliness?" asked Emma. "How is that possible?"

"Not so much loneliness as the chemicals created in the brain when a person feels isolated or lonely, disconnected from others. To The Void, this chemical is like chocolate to you humans. It communicates sort of telepathically, like voices in your head, so people don't even realize their minds have been invaded. People just think they're hearing voices, voices that encourage them to do things that end up isolating them.

"On Napori, people had already begun the process themselves, without realizing it. The society had become more and more individualized, people living apart, working long hours, forgetting about art and creativity in their drive for success and money. It was easy for The Void. It slipped right in and took over where people had already started. Napori now is completely infected. Everyone's isolated, everyone's alone. We've sent specialists to try to turn things around, but it's difficult. You can't kill The Void. All you can do is change people's behavior and actions. Things like dance, like singing. Innovation. Connection. Getting together with friends. Meeting new people. Seeing movies and making art. Playing. Those are deadly poison to The Void, and it'll leave of its own accord. But once that isolation slips in, it's hard for people to remember that they can make changes. They have to step outside their comfort zone. It's hard.

"Anyway, Dr. Waldo is pretty sure Vik is infected, and is helping The Void. The Void doesn't have a body, really, so it can only get into people's minds and make them do things. And The Void hates the Hub. The Hub is keeping The Void from spreading as freely as it would like, and The Void wants the Hub destroyed."

"So you're trying to keep Vik from destroying the Hub," said Emma.

"Exactly."

"And you're hoping to keep The Void from spreading to our Earth, too, is that why you've been there so much?"

"Oh, no," said Eve, shaking her head slowly. "No, Emma, don't you see? The Void is already there. It's been there a while."

chapter nine

Emma took this in. This thing, this horrible thing called The Void, already on Earth? She recognized the truth of it right away. People on their phones all the time, not really connecting even when they were sitting at the same table, was that The Void? Critics, both amateur and professional, incessantly judging people (and finding them failing), making people afraid to try new things, was that The Void? Social media, where it sometimes seemed everyone was begging for attention, but no one was listening, was that The Void?

Not realizing the intense impact of this revelation on Emma, Eve continued. "So, the travel, sure it's interesting, but it's also important. Besides," she said, "there's more to it. We're not just looking for Vik."

Overwhelmed by everything Eve had said so far, Emma waited for her to go on, but she didn't. Finally Emma's curiosity got the best of her.

"What?" she said. "What else are you looking for?"

Eve stared hard at Emma, judging, assessing. Emma tried arranging her features to look as trustworthy as possible. Finally, Eve spoke again.

"We're looking for my mom," Eve said.

Emma was thrown. She'd hardly had time to even wonder where

Eve's mother might be, but yes, come to think of it, where *was* Eve's mother? Emma realized she'd just assumed there had been a separation, a divorce, perhaps an untimely death. But the idea that Eve's mother could be completely missing hadn't even crossed her mind.

"Where is she?" Emma asked.

Eve laughed a cheerless laugh. "We don't know. That's why we're looking."

Emma felt a swoosh of guilt for having been jealous of Eve, for having begrudged her Ben's affection. What kind of existence could it be, after all, risking life and limb on planets such as this, planets that seemed harmless at first but then revealed angry inhabitants and untold dangers? It might be exciting at first, but to imagine that her mother might be lost on a planet somewhere? Emma shuddered at the thought.

"You see," said Eve, seeming to warm to the idea of talking about her story for once, "Mom and Dad, their relationship was always difficult. Dad says it's because they both have such strong personalities. They're both passionate, opinionated, stubborn people. They loved each other ... love each other ... but sometimes, they just clash.

"Mom was—is—a scientist. Great Aunt Doethine, my great great aunt who first discovered elevators, was one of Mom's great aunts. Mom used to go over to her house, and they'd talk all about the elevators and the discoveries and universes and life. Mom loved it. It was no surprise to anyone when she became a scientist herself.

"That's how Mom and Dad met. He's an archaeologist, see, not an interuniversal scientist. He likes staying home, on our own planet, discovering what came before us. We're still learning so much on Lero. It seems there may have been a civilization before we got there, even. Amazing, right? I mean, it makes sense. It's such a great planet."

Emma could hear the homesickness in Eve's voice, and wondered again about all the young girl had left behind to go on this quest with her father. "How many people are on your planet?" She still couldn't picture a whole other alien world, full of other people, all going about their days, falling in love, going on archaeological digs, being scientists, losing touch with family. It all sounded so very ... ordinary.

"Napori, the mother planet, has about twelve billion people. Lero only has around a hundred thousand, maybe a hundred and ten by now. We've grown a lot, but we're still small. We're trying to learn from our ancestors' mistakes, do it right this time."

Emma nodded. The chance to start over with a whole new planet, she thought, where would you even begin?

"Anyway," Eve continued. "Mom and Dad met because Mom was trying to find signs of ancient writings that might have led them to more elevators, or even something new and undiscovered. They met and fell in love and married and had me, but I was sort of a side note. Raised myself a bit, I'd say. Well, Dad helped. Mom went on a lot of expeditions. There was another scientist she went off with a lot, a man. Dad is the jealous type, or was, and he jumped to conclusions. They separated for a couple years, but they never fell out of love."

The normalcy of the story fascinated Emma. "Sounds like some people I know on Earth," she said.

"I stayed with Dad because his life was more stable, what with Mom gone all the time. I'd go on excavations and digs with him, I liked that." She smiled. "I always imagined I'd make some huge discovery that would make Mom so proud she'd come back."

The smile left Eve's face. "That hasn't happened yet." She exhaled slowly. "One day, Mom called Dad. This was about a year ago. A year of our years, that is, not yours. She said she'd discovered something."

Eve fell silent. Emma waited, impatiently. When again she couldn't stand it anymore, she asked, "What? Did she say what she'd discovered?"

Eve looked up at the girl sitting across from her and stared her straight in the eye. "We've never told anyone this. Only me, Dad, and Dr. Waldo. And I think Dad told Dr. Waldo's Secret Garden. That's it."

Emma realized she was holding her breath. "I won't tell," she said. Who, after all, would she tell? Everyone? No one? It was entirely possible she would never see another living soul again. Despite Eve's apparent confidence that they would get out of this situation they were in, this cave, this disaster, Emma was not so sure. Nothing in her past gave her any resources to get herself out of this predicament. With this realization came a rush of both overwhelming sadness, as well as determined resignation. If these were her last hours on Earth—well, on a planet—her last hours in life, she was going to make them count. "I won't say anything to anyone," she said.

Eve, understanding the situation as well, even if she didn't acknowledge it out loud, relented. "Mom called Dad to tell him she thought she'd discovered a new type of elevator, a new way to travel. That's all she said. A week later, she disappeared."

"No!" Emma gasped. "A new kind of elevator? What does that mean? Is that what happened to her? Did she take a new elevator somewhere and … get lost?"

Eve nodded. "Could be. We think so. We don't think she's on our planet. At first, we suspected the guy she was always with had hurt her, a jealous peer wanting to take credit and all that, but he was cleared. She's just gone. We think she took the new elevator somewhere. The problem is, where? If everywhere in the multiverse is a possibility, or if she discovered something beyond even the multiverse, where do you begin to look? So, we're looking for

Vik because of The Void, but also to make sure he doesn't unravel the universes, at least not before we find Mom. We're looking for Mom, too. Anything. Anything could be a sign, anywhere. We're just traveling with hope and a bunch of rocks.

"And that," she concluded, "is why Dad is so determined to find Vik."

Emma was silent. To think of losing a parent to death was bad enough. But to literally lose a parent somewhere in the vastness of everything that exists, that would be devastating. Or Charlie. As much as he drove her crazy, she wouldn't know what to do without him. He was, simply put, an extension of her own heart. And she hadn't missed Eve's statement, "something beyond even the multiverse." The idea of multiple universes was already difficult enough to comprehend. The idea of something beyond the multiverse was impossible.

"So where do you start?" asked Emma. Silently, she added, *if we ever get out of this cave alive.*

Eve reached to her neck and pulled the wishing rock pendant up from under her shirt. She then pulled up another cord from around her neck. Dangling at its end was a bright white rock, like the one Emma had found on the beach and like the one Eve wore on a ring on her finger. "This one is Mom's," she said. "It's calibrated to her energy. If we come anywhere near her, I'll know."

Emma nodded. Eve sighed. What more was there to say?

After that, they sat quietly with their loud thoughts in the small cave for long minutes that dragged into hours, waiting on the sunrise, wishing for morning or a miracle. Both of them slept a bit; both of them grew hungry. Eve pulled out high-protein energy bars for them to share. The bars were almost tasteless, with a mild coconut flavor, but mostly they provided something to chew on and revived their depleted resources.

Emma looked outside periodically, gauging the transition from darkness to light. She thought the sky seemed slightly less dark, and the app on Eve's high-tech watch confirmed it. Soon they would head out, but not yet. Emma was eager to find Charlie but did not want to get even more lost herself in the process. She had no idea how they might find the elevator again, after running away from it in such a panic. She was starting to lose hope that she'd ever see Charlie, or Ben, again.

Trying to distract herself from her growing despair, Emma struck up a lighter conversation. "So I guess people date on your planet?" she asked. "I mean, based on your Mom and Dad, it sounds like Earth, at least what you told me."

Eve shrugged. "They do. I haven't had much time. We've been running around the universes since before I turned ten."

"Ten!" said Emma. "That's forever!"

"Oh, sorry. I forgot. Ten our years. Dad and I calculated it out one time when we were stuck in the elevator. Ten in our years is maybe somewhere around sixteen and a half in your years. It's because our planet takes longer to go around our sun. Our year is longer. On our planet, we figured people live about sixty years at most, as opposed to one hundred on Earth. Based on that, we decided I'm around seventeen and a half now. But in our years, I'm not quite eleven yet. Dad's twenty-five. Dr. Waldo is ... well, I think he's around thirty."

"You got stuck in the elevator?" This news concerned Emma. "Does that happen a lot? I mean, you got stuck, and now we can't get through to the Hub ... I guess I thought with something as old as time, the bugs would be worked out?"

Eve shrugged. "It's not perfect. And sometimes, we don't know, it could just be the universes' way of protecting us from something. Have you ever noticed that, sometimes you really want something, and then later you're really glad you didn't get it? I like to think that the universes are watching out for me when that happens. So maybe when the elevator isn't working, it's for our own good."

Emma wasn't convinced that it was for their own good not to be able to get back to Dr. Waldo, or to be stuck in a cave on a planet with hostile natives, but she had to admit there were times she was glad she hadn't gotten what she wanted.

"Tell me more about what it's like on your planet," said Emma, rubbing her eyes and yawning. "If ... when we get out of here, can we go visit, maybe?"

"It's nice," said Eve, smiling wistfully. "It's beautiful. All the homes are built into the hillsides, like those hobbits your people like, from those books. That's real life for us. Because of what happened on Napori, you know. Anyway, no, I haven't dated much yet. Something to look forward to, I guess."

"Do you like Ben?" The words came out of Emma's mouth before she could stop them. More light was spilling in the crack from outside, but Emma was glad for the cover of shadows.

Eve sounded surprised. "Of course I like Ben. He's very nice. He's sweet."

"I mean, do you *like* him?"

"I don't even know how that would work," said Eve, laughing softly. "Different species? Different universes?"

"It works on Star Trek," said Emma, wondering if Eve would recognize the reference.

Eve held up her right hand and spread her fingers into a "V," two fingers on each side. "Live long and prosper," she said. "We watch that in the Hub sometimes. Well, I may be an alien girl, but Ben is not Captain Kirk. It's not that easy. I mean, talk about long distance relationships. Plus, the bracelets. They don't just make languages sound familiar. They make beings look familiar. I look more or less human, if you saw me without the bracelet. But not entirely."

Not entirely? What did she mean? Emma couldn't believe Eve would end the conversation there, but Eve didn't elaborate. Did she have two heads? Five eyes? What could "not entirely" possibly mean? Emma stared at the gleaming curve of the bracelet peeking out from under the edge of Eve's sleeve. She knew it would be wrong to rip it off Eve's arm, but nonetheless, for a very brief moment, she was tempted.

A noise outside halted her thoughts.

"What was that?" she whispered, her words hardly more than a breath of the wind. She'd become comfortable in the cave, but her senses now all became pinpoint alert.

Eve replied by shaking her head. She held up her hand to indicate "don't move," but Emma was already frozen in place.

Her brain, however, was spinning. She took a mental inventory of the weapons they had available to them. Eve must have something, mustn't she? Something that would pop out of the thing on her wrist, all 007-like? Dr. Waldo surely would not let her and Milo go traveling amongst the stars and alien creatures without self-defense of some sort. But what if Eve didn't have it with her? There were rocks on the floor of the cave, but she wasn't sure if they were loose. What did she have on her? A shoe, rather dull, no sharp edges. A firm voice, if they were facing an alien that was susceptible to guilt. Fingernails, too short. A bottle of water in her backpack.

Unless the creature was a Wizard of Oz witch that would melt if she threw some liquid on it, she was more or less defenseless.

Barely breathing, Emma peeked out of the corner of her eye at Eve. If Eve was afraid, Emma wasn't sure she'd be able to contain her own fear.

Eve looked calm. How did she look so calm? Nonetheless, she did. Alert, certainly, as though she'd suddenly generated twice as many cells and all of them were tuned to the noise outside, but still calm.

Emma decided to courage up and follow Eve's lead. Or at least, she stayed still.

After about a minute, the tension flowed out of Eve like water off a duck's back. A few seconds later, two natives of the planet appeared, followed by Charlie.

"Hey, neighbors!" said Charlie. His words were jovial but his demeanor was more reserved. Emma could sense something was wrong. "Thought we'd lost you! We were two caves over. Turns out they weren't chasing us, just trying to keep us from being eaten. Meet our new friends. I'm pretty sure I don't have their names right. This is Zadra," he said, indicating the shorter of the two aliens, who appeared to be female. "And this is Yalik." Charlie patted the taller, sturdier of the two on the back. "Lucky for us, they speak English."

Emma frowned.

Charlie pulled his sister into a tight hug. "Missed you, Emma. I'm so glad you're safe. What would I do without you?"

"I missed you too," said Emma, returning the hug. What would she do without her Charlie?

"Nice to meet you, Zadra and Yalik. Did Charlie get your names right?" asked Eve, reaching out to grasp Charlie's hand in welcome and relief.

"Close enough," said Zadra, with a grimace that might have been her version of a smile. "We were in our nighttime hunt when we saw you wandering around. It was clear you had no idea there were plassensnares behind you. We were chasing them away, not you. We apologize for scaring you."

"Plassensnares?" asked Emma.

"Sort of angry mini-mammoth-like things. Yalik drew one for us in the dirt to show us what they look like. They chased Ben and me right into our cave, and Zadra and Yalik followed, just to make sure we were safe," said Charlie. "We've been waiting over there. Yalik decided it was light enough to come out and help us."

"The plassensnares only hunt in darkness," explained Yalik.

"Zadra thought you might be over this way," said Charlie. "When we got near, it was pretty obvious. You trampled the ground pretty good."

"Charlie." Emma could not believe he was rambling on this way.

"Yes?" said Charlie.

"*Ben.* Where is Ben? You said he was with you; where is he?" The relief of having found her brother quickly turned to concern for Ben.

"Oh yes. That." Charlie looked at Yalik and Zadra as though they somehow might take over the conversation, but it was clear they were impartial observers. "Yup, okay. Well, you know that thing Dr. Waldo gave Ben, that we were only supposed to use if we found Vik, that would send him straight back to Eve's home world?"

Emma gasped. "You mean the pigeon, the device that wasn't very well tested, and on occasion *obliterated* the objects it sent to Lero?" She hoped he was not going where she thought he was going with this conversation.

"Yes. Obliterated. Yup. Well, Ben may have been looking at it in the cave, just for something to do while we were waiting for it to get light outside, and, well, he's gone."

Emma stared at Charlie. *No.* She must have misunderstood.

"Gone," said Eve. "To Lero."

"One assumes," said Charlie. "Or I guess one hopes. Better than oblivion, right? Haha?"

His attempt at humor was met with blank looks from Eve and Emma. Zadra and Yalik didn't react at all. Clearly this was a more primitive planet. The Earthlings, Eve, and the people of this planet could understand each other because of the bracelets, which was a great help, but as far as technology, it was doubtful they'd find much here. Whatever had happened to Ben had likely been far beyond their understanding. All they knew was that they'd found Charlie.

"We need Dr. Waldo," said Eve, becoming more agitated and increasingly less calm. "We have to get back to the Hub. We just have to."

"Maybe whatever was wrong with the elevator has been fixed," said Emma. It was, after all, about the only hope they had.

"Can you take us back to where we were when you first saw us?" Eve asked the natives. "It's very important that we find the right place."

Yalik nodded. "Yes." Nodding apparently meant "yes" here, too.

"Okay, let's go." Eve said.

Eve and Emma quickly re-packed their bags, then the group walked back into the lush forest, Yalik leading the way with Eve up front, and Zadra following at the back.

"She must not want us to get lost again," Charlie said to Emma.

"Did they tell you much about this place?" asked Emma, keeping her voice low.

"I didn't ask too much," said Charlie. "I didn't want to scare them by telling them we're aliens from another universe. Or maybe we're in our own universe? I don't even know. But I doubt they suspect people live on other planets. I just told them we were from another place and we were lost. They couldn't believe we didn't know about plassensnares. Weird, they don't seem bothered that we're dressed totally different from them."

"It's the bracelet, I think," said Emma. "Eve told me the bracelets also make us look like … I don't know how to explain it. We look like whoever sees us, I think. When they see us, we must look like them, just like they more or less look like us to us. And I wouldn't be surprised if they don't even know there are other planets, much less universes." said Emma. "So strange. It's like going back in time. But like Milo said, time is tricky."

Charlie just nodded.

The sun was barely up, hanging low on the horizon. Like the moons from the night before, this sun was enormous compared to Earth's sun. In the heat, steam rose from the dewy foliage and the damp ground. Yalik moved with confidence through the trees and bushes. Nothing looked familiar to Emma, possibly because of the change from moonlight to sunlight, but more likely from the fact she'd been running with blind terror at top speed when they first passed through. When they'd arrived last night, their ignorance made them feel safe. Now, flanked front and back with people who knew what dangers to watch out for, Emma felt a sense of calm. This planet, if one learned what to watch out for, was lovely and peaceful. No bathrooms, though, and no kitchen, no wi-fi ... maybe she liked her own home after all.

At the front of the group, Eve stopped. Yalik looked at her with what might have been surprise. "You are correct," he said with a grimace-smile, "this is where we found you."

"I thought so," said Eve, twirling the wishing rock pendant. "Okay, that's all we needed. Thank you so much for bringing us here. We'll be fine now."

Yalik and Zadra did not look convinced.

"No, really," said Charlie, waving. "We're good. Thank you."

Emma, Charlie, and Eve stood awkwardly, staring at Yalik and Zadra, waiting for them to leave. Finally, looking confused but again with an air of indifference, Zadra held a hand to his chest, said, "Be well," and they turned and left.

Eve waited a few minutes after the pair had disappeared into the distance. "I hope they're not watching," she said. She turned to Charlie. "Did they indicate that they saw us arrive here last night?"

"They didn't say anything," said Charlie, "but they're kind of closed-mouthed types. I didn't want to get them too suspicious so I didn't ask if they'd seen us fly in on our spaceship."

"Elevator," corrected Emma.

"I know," said Charlie. "Just joking, sis." He reached and wrapped an arm over her shoulders, but she didn't hug back.

"Can I borrow your Chapstick?" Emma asked her brother. "Something about this air has dried up my lips something awful."

"Chapstick?" Charlie said, puzzled. "I don't have any, sorry."

"Make note of that, please, to tell the committee," said Emma.

Charlie just stared at her. "What?" he said.

"No problem. Let's go," she said tersely, unraveling herself from Charlie's arm. "Before they come back."

Eve opened the door; to everyone's relief, it opened without incident. They stepped inside the room and the door closed behind them.

"That's so weird," said Charlie, shaking his head. "An invisible room in the middle of a forest. What's not weird about that? That's weird."

Eve was holding her breath. "Come on, Hub. Let us in. Please, please, please, let us in."

Emma added her own plea. "Let us in, Hub. Please, let us in." She waited to see if Charlie would add his "aliens aliens aliens" chant. He did not.

She didn't have much time to think about it. The door to the Hub slid open without hesitation. Dr. Waldo awaited on the other side, his body contorted with tension, his face twisted with concern.

chapter ten

"Thank the universes you're all back!" Dr. Waldo cried out. He swept Emma, Charlie, and Eve into a tight group hug, then released them and dropped into a chair at a table near the elevator, overwhelmed with relief. The others sat down with him. "We don't know what happened," he said. "That quake that shook just before we sent you away, Vik created that. We traced the disturbance to another universe. One of our scientists went there to investigate. It was a planet with no inhabitants, no life, totally desolated, we can at least be grateful for that. But Vik—or someone, we assume Vik—tried to blow up the elevator from the outside. He detonated so many bombs, bombs of such force, that they left a crater at least six kilometers wide around the elevator. That caused the quake all through the universes, they would have felt it on your Earth too, as we did in the Hub. Still that elevator, it is strong, didn't do a thing to it, as you know, because you left in it right afterward."

His elbows on the table, Dr. Waldo rested his head on the palms of his hands. "Luckily, Vik does not seem able to get into the Hub. We don't know what he is using for a key. He can get into the elevator, we know, but we can only hope he can't get in here. If he does … we shouldn't have let you go in the elevator without knowing what happened! We put you at such risk! We didn't know, we didn't know. But tell me, where did you go? Did you see any signs of Vik? Wait—there's an odd number of you now." He counted the people around him, pointing in turn at Eve, then Emma, then Charlie. "Where's the tall, dark-haired one? Brian?"

"Ben," said Eve. "Well, it seems we have a problem."

Charlie explained to Dr. Waldo what he'd explained to the girls, how Ben accidentally set off the device that would send a person back to Eve's planet, how he'd disappeared, how they had no idea whether Ben had made it safely to Lero. As Charlie spoke, Dr. Waldo went further into a flurry of "Oh dear"s and "Oh my"s.

"Well, children, now, don't worry," he said, though his tone definitely sounded worried. "I gave Ben the almost most recent version of the pigeon, I'm sure he's back home on Lero now, safe and sound, nothing to fret about, we just ... well, since the quake, it seems the Hub's calibrations are a tad off, as perhaps the elevator's are, from what you're telling me? Things aren't working quite right. The Hub sealed itself off from the elevator completely for a bit, self-repairing, it seems, re-setting, but we just don't know right now, I think it has fixed itself, lightning fast healing, that elevator, but we just can't be sure ..."

"The *almost* most recent version of the pigeon?" said Eve. She had watched videos of trials of early pigeon iterations. "Almost" worried her.

"Yes, well, it was only one update short of the most recent ones, just a minor glitch, no need for concern, I'm sure all is fine. We'll get in touch with our people on Lero as soon as we can get through, check in with them, I'm sure you'll see there's nothing to worry about, nothing at all," said the scientist, nervously tapping the table with his fingers.

"Dr. Waldo, that's not our only problem," said Emma. She looked at Charlie and directed her next words at him. "Did you guys really think I wouldn't figure it out?"

Charlie squirmed in his seat but smiled. "Figure what out?" he said, eyes wide with innocence.

"Dr. Waldo," Emma addressed the scientist again, "this isn't my brother. When we left here, I don't know where you meant for us to go, but we ended up on a parallel Earth, a parallel Dogwinkle Island, with another Charlie and another Emma. My Charlie and this Charlie apparently decided, for some ridiculous reason, to switch places without telling anyone." She looked at Charlie again. "Did you think I wouldn't know?"

"What gave me away?" asked Parallel Charlie, who had thought he'd been quite convincing. "We figured you guys—you and my sister—would get it eventually, but we just wanted to switch places for a while, give us each a chance to travel around. Your Charlie wanted to see our Earth, and I wanted to get off it. Just to see what it was like. No harm done!"

But Emma was neither convinced nor mollified. She lifted Parallel Charlie's arm and pulled back his sleeve to reveal the bracelet. "My Charlie is smart, giving this to you when you switched clothes. You must have been quick about that, because I don't remember your being out of our sight for long," she said.

"We did it right when we got to the lighthouse, just before we all left here." He was quite pleased with himself, as Emma knew her own Charlie would be as well. "Ran into the bathroom, switched, no one knew!"

"You left Charlie without a bracelet," Emma said. "Did you guys at least test your languages first, to see if we all speak the same English? Or did you leave him with no way to communicate?"

Parallel Charlie's face fell. Clearly, this thought had not occurred to the Charlies.

Emma continued, her fear for her own Charlie feeding her anger.

"If the elevator was broken when we left," she turned to Dr. Waldo, "do you even know where we went? How to find this Charlie's home? The parallel Earth? Can you get us there again to get my Charlie back?"

"Well, now, hmm, that's an interesting question," said Dr. Waldo, tapping more rapidly on the table, his fingers creating subconscious patterns and punctuating his thoughts. "There wouldn't be just one parallel Earth, now, would there? No, no, no, it's infinite everything, infinite parallel Earths, infinite other universes, infinite infinities, it becomes … difficult."

Emma's heart sank straight through her and into an abyss, a black hole. She could feel it, the sucking fear of loss. What if they couldn't get her Charlie back? She'd completely forgotten about the other issues at hand—whether she, or any of the rest of them, could get back home themselves; whether Ben was alive or scattered throughout the cosmos. She just wanted to find Charlie.

Eve understood how Emma felt. "Dr. Waldo, have you seen my father since we left?" she asked. "Is he okay?"

"I'm so sorry, my dear, you're the first we've seen. Well, then, that's a good sign, though, let's not despair, the Hub is repairing itself and bringing people home, sorting everyone back to their proper places, just a matter of time, it hasn't failed yet! Well, it failed a bit, but it's fixing that, isn't it! We just need to wait—"

"We *can't* wait," said Emma. "What if Charlie needs us? I need to find him." She turned to Parallel Charlie, her tone softer this time. "No offense to you. I'm sure you're lovely, but you're not my Charlie."

The young man gently punched her shoulder. "No worries, parallel sis. I get you. You're not my Emma, either."

Emma felt bad, realizing she may have been a bit harsh with this would-be brother. After all, her own brother was equally at fault—

if not more, knowing him. And she couldn't blame the Charlies. She, too, had been curious about that other Earth, the other family, and she would have understood if the other Emma had wanted to leave on an adventure. Still, she was resolved to leave immediately. "We need a plan," she said, turning to Eve.

"First, we need to find Ben, and then we need to switch the Charlies back, and then we need to get us back to my dad." Eve counted out the list with her fingers as she spoke. "Dr. Waldo, do you really think the elevator's working right again? If it is, getting to Lero should be easy. We can look for Ben, and then he can help us find Charlie."

"I can't promise anything," said Dr. Waldo, shaking his head, "but the fact you made it back here seems like a good omen." He sounded far from certain. "We've been working on new technologies, and we have a hypothesis that all beings carry a trace of their home universe in their genes. It's possible that this Charlie has within his own DNA the key to finding his universe again. And, I do say, the elevator, it is smarter than we give it credit. We are quite far from fully understanding it just yet. It might be able to help us in its own way. How, I don't know, but it might. And we've been working out new ways of traveling, nothing we're ready to give you just yet, but you can look." He held out a small black sphere he'd been carrying in his pocket. "We think we have something, a way to travel without the elevator, maybe with more precision. We were working on it just when you got here. I'd love to show you sometime, but for now I think we'd best stick with the elevator. I call it Dark MATTER: dark, because it is black, obviously, sometimes we state the obvious; and MATTER, Multiverse And Time Travel Energy Redistributer." He wiggled in his chair with delight at his own cleverness, then showed them the sphere and started to point out some features: tap here to designate coordinates; swipe here to travel.

"I understand," said Emma, anxious to get moving, "none of us can do any more than our best. Should we leave Charlie here with you to do the DNA trace, while Eve and I go get Ben?"

"No," said Parallel Charlie. "You're not going without me."

"Really, Charlie, have you not had enough adventure?" asked Emma, exasperated. "Can't you stand to stay here just this once?"

"It's dangerous out there," said Parallel Charlie solemnly. "After what I've seen, I don't want you going alone."

Emma was about to protest that she and Eve would not, in fact, be alone, and that they could very well take care of themselves, thank you very much, and what a chauvinistic thing that was to say. But she knew she wanted Charlie with them—her own Charlie, preferably, but in his absence, this Charlie would do. He wasn't so bad.

She nodded. "Okay, then. You can come."

From the Hub side, the elevator had a strange appearance: it looked like a plain rustic sliding barn door (Dr. Waldo's doing, Emma assumed), standing inside a frame of a dark-colored wood, standing inside nothing. There were no walls above it or to its sides; nothing but air. From the back, the frame was still visible but the door was not; the frame instead surrounded an expanse of empty wall. Emma was studying the frame with fascination while she, Eve, and Parallel Charlie waited for Dr. Waldo, who had been pulled away briefly by another scientist. Eve and Parallel Charlie had just joined Emma when from within the elevator, they heard a loud popping sound.

"That's odd," mumbled Dr. Waldo, rubbing his chin as he returned to the elevator. "It's generally soundproof. I've never heard any sounds coming from inside there before." Then, again—another pop, this one even louder. And another. And another.

The elevator door blasted open, flying out of the frame and nearly hitting Dr. Waldo. A young, dark-haired man stood in the empty space where there once was a door, covered in debris and dust from the explosion, a satisfied grin on his face, a giant weapon in his hands.

"Vik." Dr. Waldo neither greeted nor acknowledged the man, but just stated his name. An affirmation of the man's presence, but not a surrender.

Vik pointed the gun at Dr. Waldo.

"Sorry, old man," he said. "You know we have to destroy this place."

Emma held her breath. She felt Parallel Charlie's hand reach for hers, his fingers intertwining tightly with her own. Grateful, she squeezed back but otherwise didn't move. Out of the corner of her eye, she saw Eve. All the color had drained from the Lero girl's already pale face, but the look in her eyes was fierce. Eve would not go down without a fight.

"Vik," Dr. Waldo said again, this time addressing the young man in front of him, whose dark eyes looked crazed, possessed. "This isn't necessary, you know."

Vik's voice was calm, empty, and flat. "Dr. Waldo," he said with an air of indulgence, "you're right. It isn't necessary at all. If you leave, if everyone leaves here, our problems will be solved. You will live."

"You know we won't leave here," said Dr. Waldo, straightening his back but holding on to a chair to steady himself. "We are explorers. This Hub is meant to for discovery. This science, exploring the multiverse, this is our calling. We will not leave."

Watching as quietly as she could, Emma expected Vik to get angry, to be full of rage, but instead he spoke smoothly and slowly, a parent addressing an errant child. His cold voice was slick and slimy, like the trail of a slug. "Your calling." He nodded. "Yes. A grand, worthwhile calling, or it once was anyway. It's lonely, now, isn't it, Dr. Waldo? Don't you miss home? You've been here so long. You never leave. Everyone else comes and goes, but here, you are all alone. You know you just want to go back to Lero, see if you can rebuild your life again, after ... well, you remember. You don't have to be brave, Dr. Waldo. People will understand. Tell them you've done enough. Your work here is done. Go home."

For a moment, Dr. Waldo faltered, but he quickly regained his composure. "I know what you're doing," he said. "It won't work. That's The Void talking, Vik. Not you. It has infected you. We know what has happened and we know how to help you, Vik. You don't have to live with The Void inside you."

Dr. Waldo's words fell on deaf ears. "I'm giving you a choice here," said Vik magnanimously. "You can leave ... or you can die."

Emma heard herself gasp involuntarily. She snapped her mouth shut, but it was too late.

Still looking at Dr. Waldo, Vik paused, staring off blankly into the distance, as though he was listening to something the rest of them couldn't hear. He nodded. Smiled. Then turned to face Emma directly.

"Emma," he said, his dark eyes piercing into the young woman's soul.

She squeezed Charlie's hand tighter. How did Vik know her name?

"We know many things," Vik replied to her unspoken question. The smile on his face grew sickeningly sweet. "You know us, too, Emma. Don't be afraid. We won't hurt you."

I could just stay here and they wouldn't even notice.

"What?" said Emma. "Who said that?" She felt dizzy; glimmers of the dry planet with the two suns flashed through her mind.

"You said that, Emma. Don't be silly. Of course that was you. You're smarter than the rest of them, you know. They hold you back, don't they? Make messes you have to clean up? A waste of your time. They don't realize how smart you are. They're too busy paying attention to themselves," said Vik, taking a step toward her. *They wouldn't even notice.*

"They go off and leave you sometimes, right? We know they do. This one, she's so pretty, the boys all want to be with her? It hurts, doesn't it Emma? Don't you want to just leave all that behind? I know a way. We can help you. You don't have to feel that anymore. You're better than them. You deserve better. You ... are special."

It hurts. I'm special. I deserve better. "I just ... I mean ..." Emma's mind was reeling, so many voices inside, so much noise ... she just wanted it to stop, she just wanted to be alone ...

No, Emma, don't you see? The Void is already there. It's been there a while.

"It's you!" yelled Emma. "You're in my head! Get out! What do you want? Get out! Get out!" She shook her head violently to rid herself of the voices she felt invading her brain. "Stop! I know what you're doing! Stop!"

"Vik," said Dr. Waldo, reaching out to the young man, "you've lost yourself. Come back. I have people who can help you. We can help you get rid of The Void—"

"No!" cried out Vik, turning back to Dr. Waldo and lifting the weapon to his shoulder. "You cannot trick me! I was lost without The Void. You at the Hub would destroy us! No more negotiating! You had your chance!"

As Vik spoke, fury raging in his eyes, Dr. Waldo rolled the Dark MATTER sphere over to Eve. She caught it and looked at Dr. Waldo in confusion.

"Anywhere, Eve!" he cried. "Link arms, and swipe! Go anywhere but here!"

Vik cocked his weapon and pointed it into the Hub.

"GO!" Dr. Waldo yelled to the teens, throwing all his weight and all his strength behind himself as he flew at Vik, attempting to tackle him if it was the last thing he ever did.

Emma, Eve, and Parallel Charlie linked arms and held hands for dear life. Eve swiped a finger across the sphere, with not the slightest idea what would happen next.

What they experienced was worlds—universes—apart from the elevator's boot-in-mud-sucking, metal-smoke-honey-scented trip. Instead, the three fell into nothingness, tumbling without bodies or space around them. They could feel themselves disappear, fading from the edges, until all that remained was a breath and a heartbeat. Complete silence. Empty nothingness, but with awareness, somehow, an awareness that was, separately and also together, Emma, Eve, and Parallel Charlie. In the micro instant of nothingness, Emma could feel the Hub. She could feel the everythingness that was the Hub, the infinite possibilities, all the universes within her and herself within all the universes, the point where everything blended and everything was possible, and for a moment she understood. Understood how to travel to the ends and to the beginnings, how to be anywhere and everywhere; she knew the answers without even knowing the questions. Then, quickly as it had started, she could feel her body coming back starting at the core, out to the edges, she was a thought, then a whisper, then a puff, then a being again, still somehow holding tight to Eve and Parallel Charlie, still alive.

They were somewhere.

At first, it took them a few moments to remember how to breathe and to see and to exist. The world around them seemed ephemeral and hazy. Emma blinked hard, trying to get her eyes to settle back into their sockets, but soon she realized the haziness was not in her vision, but rather in the landscape around her. Neither a fog nor dust but rather almost a film, a layer of thickness to the atmosphere, giving the air substance beyond what Emma was used to on Earth. Emma took a breath in; the air was breathable but somehow felt heavy on her lungs. She could feel the air's weight pressing in on her from the outside; they could walk through it, but they could feel the air parting as they made their way through, as with water.

"It's the ghost universe," said Eve, her words forming slowly, hanging in the air like a cartoon caption, as language and the ability to speak re-shaped themselves in the wake of their travel. "We've landed in the ghost universe."

"The ghost universe?" said Emma. "But … does that mean we're … dead?"

Eve looked at her, but had no answer.

chapter eleven

"At least we landed on solid ground," said Eve, quietly, once they'd regained their senses and reliable use of their limbs. She held up the black sphere. Whereas before it was smooth and new, it now looked as if it was burned from the inside out, the black surface charred and flaking.

"Did we break it?" asked Parallel Charlie.

"It was a prototype," said Eve. "Who knows. It doesn't look like we can use it again, though."

The enormity of the situation did not escape any of the trio.

Nor had the newcomers' presence gone unnoticed by the denizens of the ghost planet they'd landed on. Wispy, willowy, half-there creatures of all kinds gave them a wide berth at first, gazing on them from afar with an aura of patience. All the time in the world, these creatures' movements seemed to indicate. We have no need to rush, we have nothing but time. Now, however, the more curious, the more bold, the more devious, perhaps, were starting to come closer.

A soft warm breeze swirled around the teens, gentle but unremitting. Emma shivered. She looked down at her arm: the bracelet was still there. She had no idea whether any of its components worked at this point, but she traced a finger over the amber stone, willing it to give her breath for as long as she needed to breathe here. She remembered well Dr. Waldo's ominous warning about visiting the ghost universe: "People who stay there too long can't return," he'd said. "Not a good idea," he'd admonished.

And yet, here they were.

"Eve," Emma whispered with urgency, "is there an elevator here? Dr. Waldo said it's not good to come here. We need to leave." She felt jittery just being there, far from the languid calm of the permanent residents.

"I don't think our elevator will work right now. I don't know what Vik did in there, but my guess is the elevator will need a good bit of time to fix itself again. If we could even find it, that is; if it even still exists," Eve added bleakly.

The idea sent a chill down Emma's spine. If Vik could destroy one elevator, no doubt he'd start destroying them all. She needed to find Charlie, they needed to find Ben, and everyone needed to get home.

"Aren't there more elevators, though? You said there are dozens on our planet, maybe that's the case here? If there's one, shouldn't there be more?" she asked.

"That's true," Eve said. "Where there's one elevator, usually there are several." Her voice had a note of hesitation in it.

"Usually?" Something about the word didn't encourage Emma's confidence.

"Yes," Eve sighed. "The ghost universe is different from the others we've seen. The ghost universe is kind of like the thirteenth floor on your planet. Not every elevator stops here. As far as we know, the elevator that links to your island could be the only one."

"As far as we know," Emma repeated. There were those words again. Emma longed for nothing more than a little bit of certainty at this point. "Great. The only elevator we know of has been blown up, so we couldn't use it now even if we could find it. The Dark MATTER thing is burned out. Can we still use it, though? I mean, we have to try, right?"

As they were speaking, a ghost glided nearer and nearer. Emma subconsciously brushed the air in front of her face, as though swiping at an invisible spider web. When she went on picnics, the sight of one ant would make her skin crawl for the rest of the afternoon as she imagined phantom ants crawling all over her. This was like that, though here the phantoms were made of death.

The ghost that was approaching them looked like a woman, human-like in form, though not all the ghosts were. She wasn't all gray and white, but neither was she full-color. She looked faded, somewhat transparent. Not like Dr. Waldo's Experimental Building, which was solid one minute and gone the next, but rather something like slightly murky water: see-through, but still with her own structure and matter. The woman had short hair, cut in a bob, that looked like it must have been blonde or gray when the woman was alive. She was wearing a long loose flowing dress—many of the ghosts were, whether man or woman or other—with sleeves that came down to her wrists. The hem of the dress came to just above her toes, revealing the fact that she did not quite walk but rather glided through space, almost as though stepping out didn't actually move her forward but rather indicated the direction in which she wanted to propel herself.

The ghost floated nearer and nearer. Her gaze on the invaders didn't waver as she approached, unblinking. She seemed neither threatened nor threatening, but yet very intense.

When the ghost spoke, Emma nearly jumped out of her skin.

"Helloooooooo," said the ghost, her lips turning up in to the vaguest hint of an amused smile. "Did we get lossst?" Her voice, echoing and meandering through the thick air, sounded as though it were coming through liquid, distant and murmuring. Emma found herself straining to hear. She stepped closer to the ghost woman without realizing it.

"We're sort of lost," she said. "We're not supposed to be here." Emma sneezed.

"Noooo," said the ghost, her thin willowy shape drifting and shifting in the breeze. "Not yet. It is nice here, though, young lady. Maybe you will stay." It wasn't a question but rather a statement. "It is very nice here." The woman drifted in circles around the trio, studying them. At length, she nodded. "I seeeeeee." she said.

"Do you—" Emma sneezed again. "Excuse me. Do you know if there's a way for us to leave? We're supposed to be somewhere else."

The woman's amused smile grew. "We allllll say that when we get here. None believes she is meant to be here, but meant to be here we are." Other ghosts started to come closer.

"No, but we're *really* not supposed to be here. We're not dead," said Emma. "Right? I mean, you can tell we're not dead, right?"

The woman looked Emma up and down, painfully slowly, top of her hair to tip of her toes, missing nothing. Emma could almost feel the woman's gaze on her, like a laser through the fog. Emma sneezed, three times, in rapid succession.

"Nooo, you are not dead. Give yourself tiiiime," said the apparition. Then without another word or a backward look, the woman glided away.

Parallel Charlie watched the woman disappear, then looked at Emma. "Are you allergic?"

"What?" said Emma, sneezing.

"Ghosts. Are you allergic to ghosts?"

"What in the world are you talking about?" Sneeze, sneeze.

"We can see ghosts on our Earth, you know," he said. "Can't you see them on yours? You look like you've never seen a ghost before.

And I'd say you're allergic. Not unheard of. My mom is allergic, too. It's genetic. Emma and I got vaccinated when we were babies. The other Emma. Not you. Obviously."

"Obviously. You can see ghosts on your Earth?" Emma paused. Sneezed. "Okay, fine, you can see ghosts in Minsota. But a ghost allergy? A ghost vaccine? That's ridiculous." Sneeze. "How can a person be allergic to ghosts?"

"Ghosts are made up of different elements than people. When you die, you get mixed up with other stuff in the universe. Ghosts have aeternitum, usually some pacium, and sometimes paenitine. Live people can be allergic to any of those, especially paenitine."

Parallel Charlie's words meant nothing to Emma. "Aeternitum? Pacium? Paenitine?" she repeated. Was he just making these up?

"Don't tell me your Earth hasn't identified those elements yet?" He shook his head with exaggerated sadness. "Clearly our Earth is better. You know, from the Latin roots. Aeternitas, eternity. Pacum, peace. Paenitet, regret. Ghosts have those mixed in, in some random measure. The goal is to become a ghost with lots of pacium, not as much paenitine."

Emma sneezed. *Live people are especially allergic to paenitine,* she repeated in her head. Paenitet, regret. *The multiverse may be chaotic,* she thought, *but some things make sense.* "Are they just hanging around everywhere, your ghosts?" she asked. "Do the ghosts of your family travel with you? Did you bring them to the island with you?"

Parallel Charlie laughed. "Don't be silly, Em! No, they don't travel with us! Where would we put them in the car?"

This alternative Charlie shared a sense of humor with her own Charlie—strange and off-beat—which gave Emma a sense of safety. She started laughing, which turned into a fit of sneezes. "I guess you couldn't very well tie them to the roof of the car, either," she said, in an effort to lighten her own mood.

"Right?" said Parallel Charlie. "So look, I'm used to these ghosts, no worries, we'll be okay. They're just dead people. Or—" he paused, watching something very not-human-like glide by, "—or, they're dead, anyway."

The curious cloud of ghosts swarmed closer, carrying with it a muddled hum of interest.

"They're making me nervous," said Emma, squirming.

"Me too," said Eve. "We can see ghosts on Lero, too, but never this many at once. It's a bit disconcerting." She shuddered, then composed herself. "Okay. Let's see … I guess, let's see if we can find someone who can help."

"I don't suppose there's a Visitor Center?" said Parallel Charlie.

"Doubtful," said Eve, "but you never know. Stranger things have happened."

Indeed they have, thought Emma.

Not sure what else to do, Eve, Emma, and Parallel Charlie began walking. An occasional building or structure made from large stones dotted the landscape, but for the most part, the ghost planet was undeveloped. Ghosts wandered around seemingly without aim; some gathered in groups for exchange of ghostly gossip, while others roamed alone. There were no roads, but neither was there much vegetation to block their way. The few shrubs they could see seemed almost out of place. When they came near one, Emma reached out to touch its needles.

"It's plastic!" she said, recoiling as though the shrub had stung her.

"Makes sense, I suppose," said Eve.

"It does?" said Parallel Charlie.

"Nothing living," said Eve. "Planet of ghosts."

"But what about dead trees? Couldn't they come here too?" asked

Emma. Her sneezing continued in fits and starts. Maybe she was allergic to ghosts after all?

Eve just shrugged. The planet was as much a mystery to her as to the others.

The trio wandered for what felt like hours. Emma could feel her sense of time slipping away from her. Had they just arrived, or had they been here for days? Or perhaps, perhaps this was now home? She struggled to keep her mind clear, but her brain started to feel like the air: full of something, some thickness, imperceptible and yet undeniably there. As the fog in her mind grew, Emma started to feel warm and light, almost like she was floating. Life on the ghost planet might be rather nice, she thought. No worries, no school, no romantic entanglements to fret over, just this calm, peaceful feeling of drifting through a world without barriers. She was still walking but felt she might soon be able to glide, just as the ghosts did. She could feel the molecules of her body blending with the air, exchanging places, herself becoming more air and the air becoming more Emma. It was good.

Eve, too, was getting a glazed, blissful look on her face. Her movements became more slow, measured, serene. Only Parallel Charlie seemed to remain immune to the numbing effects of the ghost planet ... so far.

Eventually, they came to a small hill, at the top of which sat a long, low building. Like the other structures they'd seen, this was made of stones, similar to tumbled-smooth river stones, but enormous, each stone the size of a couch cushion. The entrance, an opening about five feet wide and a dozen feet high, had no door blocking inside from outside. There were no windows.

"I guess we go in?" Eve said in a lulled state of uncertainty.

Parallel Charlie led the way up the hill and into the building.

Inside the entranceway, a ghost man sat behind a stone table. His face twisted into an amused smile much like that of the woman they'd met earlier. "You found your way here," he said, with no questions about who they were or what they were looking for.

"Do you know who we are, then?" asked Parallel Charlie.

"No," said the man.

"Then what do you mean by 'you found your way here'?" asked Parallel Charlie.

"Everyone finds a way here eventually," the man said, enigmatically.

The planet's sedation continued to hold its grip on Eve and Emma, but Parallel Charlie still had a clear head. "Who is everyone?" he challenged.

"All who come here," said the man, unperturbed, his amused smile unwavering.

As he spoke, two figures appeared behind him, materializing out of the thick air, first just a ripple, then a wave, then fully present phantoms.

"Grandpa?" said Emma.

"Aunt Doethine?" said Eve.

Parallel Charlie had been unable to pull Eve and Emma away from the ghosts of their dead relatives. From what he could glean from talking with the rather unresponsive man at the desk, new arrivals to the planet gathered at this building to reunite with whichever of their loved ones might have made it to the planet before them.

"Is this the only planet ghosts come to?" Parallel Charlie had asked.

"No," the succinct man had said.

"Does everyone find someone here that they know?"

"Not everyone."

"Do you have, like, a list of people or something?"

"Or something."

"Is there anyone I know here?"

"Yes."

"Are they coming to see me?"

"Not yet."

"Why?"

"It is not time."

Parallel Charlie had felt somewhat relieved at that.

"Can we get off this planet?"

"Yes."

"How?"

The question had been met with an amused smile, and silence.

"Do you know how we can get off this planet?"

"Yes."

"Tell me how!" The ghost man's nonchalant demeanor had begun to seriously irritate Parallel Charlie.

The man had just smiled.

Parallel Charlie had given up. Now, he waited, sitting on a slab of stone, agitated, while Eve and Emma gabbed on with their relatives in the planet's leisurely manner. He didn't know why he hadn't been affected by the planet's lulling effect—maybe the ghost vaccine, he thought—but whatever the reason, he didn't want to test it much longer. He had no idea at all how long they'd been there. Hours, days, weeks, months. Years. It could already be too late, for all he knew. Emma was starting to look a little less solid. Eve had a glowy look about her. Parallel Charlie periodically looked at his arm to make sure he was still all there.

The grandfather Emma was talking to was, of course, Parallel Charlie's grandfather too, in a manner of speaking, except for the fact that on Parallel Charlie's Earth, this grandfather was still alive. Somehow, all three of them—Emma, Parallel Charlie, and the grandfather—had known that this grandpa was Emma's but not truly this Charlie's. Therefore, grandfather and granddaughter had gone off to reminisce about family trips and gatherings, the peach tree in their backyard, the giant horse trough they'd used as a swimming pool when Emma was a toddler. Eve and her great aunt were talking about elevators, and Eve's eyes glimmered with slow delight as she listened to her great aunt's mesmerizing tales.

Parallel Charlie tried again.

"How long can we stay here?" he asked the man at the counter.

"As long as forever," said the man.

"I mean, how long can we stay here before we can't leave anymore? Dr. Waldo says we might not be able to leave if we stay too long."

"This is true," said the man.

"So how much longer do we have?"

"Time is tricky."

Parallel Charlie wanted to punch something, but everything around him was stone. He didn't know what was happening, or why it wasn't happening to him, but he could tell Eve and Emma were falling under the trance of the ghost universe. If they were going to get away, they were going to have to do something. And he was going to have to take the lead.

But what to do? Parallel Charlie rubbed his eyes. He wished someone else were around to help him think. He'd never traveled around on other planets before, much less other universes. If only Ben were still with them—

"That's it!" Parallel Charlie said out loud. "The pigeon!" For better or for worse, it might be their only chance.

He walked over to Eve, who was lost in conversation with her great aunt and barely noticed his presence. Normally Parallel Charlie wouldn't be so rude as to go through another person's things, but desperate times called for desperate measures. He picked up Eve's backpack and started pulling out its contents one by one. Water, provisions, some random gadgets, and then, there it was, just the same as the one Ben had activated by mistake. The pigeon that would take them all home. Well, to Eve's home. But it was, at the very least, preferable to this place.

Eve may not have been aware of Parallel Charlie's actions, but Great Aunt Doethine was. She looked up at Parallel Charlie and nodded her approval, a look he understood to mean that it was, in fact, time for them to go. As he hastily tossed Eve's possessions back in her bag, Doethine touched Eve on the shoulder and guided her attention to the young man.

Eve, seeing what Parallel Charlie held in his hand, shrugged off the sluggish feeling and shook herself to attention. "Yes. Yes, good idea, Charlie. We need to go. Where is Emma?" she said, looking around as she fought her way out of her daze.

Emma, however, was still lost in a ghostly stupor, talking warmly with her beloved grandfather, sneezing fiercely on occasion but not seeming to notice. Parallel Charlie pulled Emma up to her feet, lifting under her shoulders. He could tell they needed to act quickly. The grandfather did not seem perturbed, either, but Parallel Charlie did not want to somehow incite a ghost riot. He linked elbows with Eve to his left and Emma to his right, squeezing tight with his arms but keeping his hands free to operate the pigeon. The glaze settling back over Eve's eyes told him she was quickly losing her focus again. Emma, too, was slipping. Parallel Charlie pushed the critical button on the pigeon, but in the split second before he did so, Emma sneezed and involuntarily let go of his arm.

chapter twelve

Parallel Charlie sat up, discombobulated and dazed. Where was he? What had happened? He heard warbly, distorted voices in the distance. He felt groggy … was the ghost universe finally getting to him? No, no, it was coming back to him. The pigeon. There was a pigeon … and Eve … and Emma. He rubbed his eyes and looked around. There was Eve, lying next to him, still knocked out. But where was Emma?

"Eve!" he cried, shaking the young woman on the floor. "Eve, wake up! Where's Emma?"

Eve rolled slowly to her side, putting a hand to her eyes to shield them from the bright overhead light. "It's okay! It's okay! He's okay!" she called out suddenly.

"What's okay? Who's okay? Eve, where's Emma?" said Parallel Charlie, confused and growing more concerned.

"No, I'm talking to them," Eve said, pointing weakly at the space beyond the glaring pool of light around them.

Parallel Charlie finally took note of their surroundings. He and Eve were on a raised circular platform in the middle of a room. The platform measured about eight feet in diameter, and was surrounded from base to the ceiling by a thick Plexiglas-like cylinder. He did not know where they were, but he knew this: they were trapped.

Outside the clear barrier, a dozen or more uniformed people stood staring at them, watching them intently.

"Eve," Parallel Charlie whispered. "Eve, where are we?"

She sat up and waved at the uniformed people. "We're on my planet. We're on Lero. You used my pigeon. That pigeon is programmed to bring people here, to this platform, inside this enclosure, so they can't escape. It's meant for Vik. We're in our version of a police station." She smiled. "You brought us to jail. But you brought us home. Good thinking." She looked around and her brows furrowed. "Wait. Where's Emma?"

"That's what I asked you. Where's Emma?" But Parallel Charlie feared he knew the answer. "I think ... I think she sneezed right when I pushed the button and she let go of me. I think ... she might still be back on the ghost planet."

Eve crumpled back to the ground. Outside the container, people murmured and moved about, but their words were indistinct.

"No," said Eve. "No. This is not how it's supposed to be."

A voice came through the barrier from speakers in the ceiling. "Eve," said the voice. "Eve, is this Vik with you?"

Eve looked up at the speakers. "No, this is not Vik. This is Charlie. Charlie, meet my people. People, meet Charlie."

Parallel Charlie looked around and found a man at a desk, speaking into a microphone. He guessed that must be the person addressing them. His suspicion was confirmed when the voice came through again as the man's lips moved. Forcing a toothy grin, Parallel Charlie waved at the man.

"Are you sure, Eve? He's not trying to get you to trick us?"

Eve stood up. "Positive." She called out to the people in the room, "Can you let us out? We've been in the ghost universe. I have no idea how long we were there. I'm a little hungry and a lot tired."

The clear cylinder rose silently into the ceiling, high enough for them to get out. Eve stepped down from the platform, and Parallel Charlie followed. The uniformed man who had been speaking through the microphone came to meet them. "Your friend, Ben, he's here too. Got here a couple days ago."

"Ben? He's here? Oh, thank goodness." Eve's voice was filled with relief.

"Yeah. We weren't sure what to do with the kid so we've been housing him at the station for the time being. I'll have someone get him while we find something for you kids to eat. And," he added, looking critically at the haggard state of their attire, "maybe a shower and a change into clean clothes."

Eve nodded her consent. Parallel Charlie was wide-eyed with curiosity. "So this is Lero," he said, his mouth gaping. "It's like both ancient and future Earth." The secure cylinder they'd landed inside was sleek and modern, but the room that housed it was distinctly rustic. The room seemed to be burrowed out of the ground; the walls were reminiscent of the dirt and stone caves they'd holed up in on the planet with the plassensnares, or the homes he'd heard about in the outback in the country of Australis back on his own planet, where people built homes underground in an effort to escape the blistering heat. The chiseled walls gave a cozy, secure feeling to the room, but the furniture and various technology—too advanced to be called computers, even—were proof of a more developed civilization.

The room itself was large, with bright lights giving off a warm sunlight-like glow, allowing the room to escape from what could have been a gloomy cavern feel. The perfectly vertical, somewhat rust-colored walls rose up and flowed into a gentle curve that joined the smooth sides to the high ceiling. Veins of a dark blue gemstone traced rivers through the face of the walls. Some openings in the walls led to hallways or further rooms; others were blocked by tightly fitting doors, hiding unknown and intriguing mysteries. There were no windows, but large screens on several walls displayed slowly rotating scenes of the Lero sky and its lush landscape, offering onlookers a serene view of the peaceful world outside. The furniture in the room somehow managed to look tidy and stylish, while also blending with the natural look of the room.

The officer led Eve and Parallel Charlie through one of the openings to a comfortable sitting area with couches covered in a forest-green fabric, and a low, round, glass-topped table. As they sat, a woman brought them a large pot filled with a hot tea-like beverage, a platter of food and some plates, and some utensils made of a silver-gray metal, perhaps titanium. The knife was recognizable as a knife. The other utensil was like a fancy spork. Parallel Charlie laughed.

"Sporks? I cross planets and universes and I get a spork?" he said to Eve, a twinkle in his eyes. He watched her for cues on the proper way to eat whatever this food was before them. A thick slice of what he supposed was some sort of meat was drizzled with a burgundy-colored sauce. The greens were clearly meant to be a salad, made of the leaves of something he didn't recognize but which he found to be inoffensive. Mixed into the salad were a variety of nuts, seeds, and chunks of some sort of vegetable.

"Why have two utensils when you only need one?" said Eve, delighted to be reunited with the food of her homeland. She eagerly dug into the meat, slicing it and smearing it in the mysterious sauce before putting it into her mouth with a look of bliss.

Parallel Charlie decided hunger would flavor whatever he was about to eat, and dug in. "Tastes like chicken," he said of the meat, laughing at his own humor. He nudged Eve. "Tastes like chicken? No?"

But Eve's attention had shifted away from the food: another officer had just brought Ben into the room to meet them.

"Ben!" she said, almost dropping her plate of food in her haste to put it down, stand up, and rush over to embrace the young man in a tight hug. "Oh, Ben! I was worried for you! You're alive! We haven't tested those pigeons much. Ours about knocked us out. I'm relieved to see you in one piece! Did it hurt when you transported?"

Ben hugged Eve back and gave her a kiss on the forehead. "I could not be happier to see you, Eve of the Lighthouse!" he said, swinging Eve around gently. "That pigeon, that should come with a warning! I was holding it, fidgeting, I guess, nervous energy. I was a little scared, I'll admit it. I don't know what happened. I must have pushed a button without realizing it. Next thing I knew, I was here. They tell me I was on that platform for a couple hours before I came to." He shook his head at the memory. "Scared me to death. I had no idea where I was or what had happened. In the time before I woke up, these officers were able to scan me to make sure I wasn't Vik, so at least I didn't wake up to guns in my face. Oh, man, am I glad you're here. I am so glad you guys are here."

"I'm so glad we found you," said Eve, clinging tight to his arm. "Everything has been so crazy, Ben. You won't believe what all has happened."

"I can only imagine! Craziest days I've ever had, that's for sure. Hey, where's Emma?" asked Ben, looking around. "Bathroom? Man, those bathrooms are weird! I had to have someone explain a few things," he laughed.

Eve and Parallel Charlie looked at each other.

"Sorry, no bathroom jokes," said Ben. When Eve and Parallel Charlie didn't respond, his joviality turned to concern. "What?" he asked. "What is it? What's wrong? Where is Emma? Is she okay? She's alive, right?"

"Ben," said Eve, "...we don't know."

"You don't know? What do you mean you don't know?" asked Ben, looking at Parallel Charlie.

Parallel Charlie explained. "We were in the ghost universe—you know, the one Dr. Waldo said not to go to. Well, long story, but Vik got into the Hub—"

"Vik got into the Hub? Are you kidding me?" said Ben. "What happened?"

"Not kidding you. Vik got into the Hub, and Dr. Waldo gave us this thing he called 'Dark MATTER,' a new gadget he's designed to travel without elevators, and, well, we ended up in the ghost universe. We don't know what happened to Dr. Waldo or the Hub, and we haven't been able to get back in. Turns out Emma is allergic to ghosts, though. Right when I activated the pigeon to come here, she sneezed, let go of me. We don't know what happened."

"Allergic to ghosts? She's still on the ghost planet?"

"We think so," said Eve. "We hope so."

"You hope so? Meaning what?" asked Ben.

"Meaning if she's not there," said Eve, "we have no idea where to look."

"It's *just* like a hobbit planet! Hobbits! Hobbits, hobbits, hobbits!" said Parallel Charlie with delight, as he, Eve, and Ben trudged back to the elevator they hoped would reconnect them with either the Hub or one of the two Earths, so they could start to make things right again.

After Eve and Parallel Charlie had finished eating, taken showers, and changed clothes, Eve and Parallel Charlie had filled Ben in on everything—including the fact that Charlie and Parallel Charlie had switched places.

"Good ol' Emma, figuring that out," Ben had said, smiling. "Can't fool her."

Ben and Parallel Charlie had conferred and found that both Earths had produced authors by the name of John Ronald Reuel Tolkien (known on one planet as J.R.R. Tolkien and on the other as John Tolkien), and that these authors had both produced epic and phenomenally successful books about Middle Earth. Both had agreed that Eve's planet was reminiscent of how The Shire—the hobbits' home—might look. With rare exceptions, all buildings on this planet were burrowed into the ground. As a result, the entire landscape with a low, natural profile, barely disturbed by civilization. Rather than the concrete prevalent on Earth and, according to Eve, on Napori, pathways and roadways here were made of permeable surfaces, letting the rain soak through and helping prevent erosion.

"We destroyed Napori," said Eve, "so we've been more careful here. Napori is paved over, built up sky high. The planet is suffocating. We're trying to avoid that here, but it's not easy."

"Where's your house?" asked Parallel Charlie, kicking a small stone ahead of him as he walked. "You must live somewhere."

Eve frowned. "Right now we're living in the Hub," she said, "which I guess makes me homeless, unless we can get back in. When we started out on this search for Vik, Dad put everything into storage and sold the house." Tugging her jacket around her despite the fact it was not cold outside, she fell silent.

Homeless. The word struck Parallel Charlie, who hadn't quite thought of it that way. But, he realized, if they couldn't find a way to get him and Ben back to their own Earths, they might meet a similar fate: living out their lives on Lero. Looking around at the beautiful area, he thought it might not be so bad. But he would miss Emma. Either Emma. Preferably his own, but if not that Emma, then the other. He needed Emma around to keep him grounded.

"I really hope Dr. Waldo is alive," said Eve, slowing to a stop.

"There it is," she said.

Ben and Parallel Charlie stopped by her side. "Where?" said Ben. Ahead of them was another low hill with a door tightly fitted in one side. "It's a hill. I thought she found the first one in an elevator?"

"She did. Well, we call them elevators still, old Napori habit, I suppose. But they're the opposite, really. Ground floor is at the top. They take you down into the ground instead of up a building. And technically, I suppose what Aunt Doethine found was *next to* an elevator, but she called it an elevator, and the name stuck."

"But it's a hill?" said Charlie, still confused.

"It used to be an elevator that went down to an old storage area that isn't used anymore. It wasn't even in use anymore when Aunt Doethine found it. Remember, the elevator portals don't appear unless you have the key. Once we're inside, we'll see it. Here, the elevators are mostly in fields, though. It's a wonder Aunt Doethine ever found this."

"How did she find it?" asked Ben.

"The day before, she'd been at a beach. She used to like to go to the beach to think. She'd walk for hours, up and down the shore-line, gathering rocks and tossing them into the ocean as her mind worked on whatever problem she was trying to solve. That day, she was thinking intensely about universes and travel, and the fact that most Leroians have never been to Napori. We've all lost touch with our ancestors and the relatives who stayed behind, because travel to Napori is just impractical for many, impossible for most. She was born long ago enough that when she was a child, the elders in the community still talked about Napori a lot. She had it in her mind that she wanted to go there, to somehow create a bridge between Lero and Napori. Anyway, while she was at the beach, she picked up one rock—I'm sure you can guess, it was a wishing rock. People make wishes on them here, too. She was about to toss it into the ocean, but then something made her keep it. She tucked it into her jacket pocket and went on with her day.

"She forgot all about the rock. The next day, she was out here in this field when it started raining, just a complete downpour. She saw this door and slipped inside to wait it out." Eve opened the door on the hill and ducked inside, motioning for Ben and Parallel Charlie to follow her. Once inside, Eve led them to the other end of the room.

"Oh, cool! I can feel it," said Parallel Charlie. "The air is vibrating." He held up the wishing rock that hung on the cord around his neck. "Nice job, rock!"

"I can feel it, too," said Ben. "That is such a weird feeling. I can imagine your great aunt would have been intrigued when she first felt this." He held out his arms, moving them in the air to test the vibrations, as though feeling around for a force field.

Holding the wishing rock pendant in her hand, Eve took one more step toward the wall. The elevator appeared before them, a large sliding door within a solid stone frame, where before there had been nothing but a wall. "You're right. She felt that vibration, and investigated around the room. She saw this."

Eve stepped up to the elevator door. It slid open before her. She peered warily through the doorway, fearful of what she might find, but all appeared in order. "It's self-healing," she explained, forgetting Dr. Waldo had already explained this. "It seems to be okay …" She stepped inside and motioned once again at Ben and Parallel Charlie to follow her. They obediently obliged, joining her in the small but seemingly intact space.

The door slid shut behind them. By habit, Eve's hand reached for the light switch, and she turned on the light.

"Let us into the Hub, please, elevator?" she implored, looking at the back wall and hoping for it to open up into the space beyond, where everything was possible.

Nothing happened.

"Please?" Eve said weakly.

The wall stood intact and unmoving, guarding the Hub, or whatever was left of it.

Eve sighed.

"Okay, well, we've at least got to get one of you home," she said quietly. "Let's start with you, Ben. We'll go to your Earth and find Dad. Maybe he'll have an idea." She didn't mention that she had no idea what universe Parallel Charlie came from, and therefore no idea how to get him home.

Before leaving the police station, Eve had contacted some of Dr. Waldo's colleagues on Lero. Not wanting to land herself and her friends on the wrong planet again, she had asked them to confirm the correct coordinates of Ben's Earth, which they had done. Eve now plugged those coordinates into the panel on the wall of the elevator.

With a chug and a sputter and a start, like the elevator was stiff from sitting too long, it started up. Smoke, metal, honey. The dizziness.

The door opened. Before them stood the familiar lobby of the Balky Point lighthouse, looking as plain and undisturbed as if they'd never left.

"Home," said Ben. "Well, that was anticlimactic, relatively speaking. But maybe we've had enough adventure for a while. Good job, Eve."

"Looks like home, anyway," said Parallel Charlie. "Yours or mine. But probably yours."

"I hope so," said Eve. She wasn't ready to celebrate just yet.

Feeling dejected, they began the long trek back to Ed's cabin. They walked in silence, dreading the moment they would have to tell Emma and Charlie's parents they'd come home without the twins.

About a mile into the route, Parallel Charlie spoke. "You know," he said, "so far, you couldn't tell which Earth it is. Looks just the same as my Earth. Or probably a million other Earths. This route looks exactly like it does on the island I came from."

Eve shot him a withering look.

"I am, however," Parallel Charlie continued, "one hundred percent confident you brought us to the right place." And he didn't speak again.

Gauging by the position of the sun and the heat of the day, it was late in the afternoon. When they'd first left Earth, it had been late morning. Eve had tried to get them back on the day they'd left, but with the state of the elevator there was no way to know yet whether they were there on the same day or even the same century. Ben, the only one with intimate knowledge of the island, didn't travel this particular road enough nor pay enough attention to the height of the trees or other potentially telling clues to have any idea whether they'd returned to their own time.

"Looks right," he shrugged, his uncertainty clear.

And so a few minutes later, when they heard a car coming up the road, they hesitated. If they were in the wrong decade—or century—they might arouse suspicion. Should they duck behind a tree? Run back to the lighthouse? Before they could decide, the car came into view.

"That's Ed's truck!" said Ben, squinting to see the white pickup more clearly in the distance. Ed was driving, Milo sat in the passenger seat, and it looked like there was someone else in the back of the extended cab ...

Seeing the teens, Ed brought the truck to an abrupt stop, stirring up a choking cloud of dirt. Eve ran through the dust to the pas-

senger side of the pickup, reaching it just as her father opened the
door. She fell into his arms.

"Dad!" she cried. "Oh, Dad! We found you! Dad, it's all wrong!
It's all gone wrong!"

Milo hugged Eve tightly. Ed looked at Ben and Parallel Charlie
(not knowing it was not the real Charlie), and his face grew puzzled
with concern. "Dr. Waldo told us you'd lost Ben. But Ben's here.
Where's Emma? What happened to Emma?" he asked. He wasn't
sure he wanted to hear the answer.

Ben and Parallel Charlie looked at each other, wondering who
would speak. Parallel Charlie realized that although this was not
his Earth and the missing Emma was not his sister, the task was his.

"Lost. We lost her. We need to find Dr. Waldo, or we're hoping
maybe Milo—"

As he spoke, the shadow from the back of Ed's truck stepped out
of the vehicle.

Eve caught the movement out of the corner of her eye. "Dr. Waldo!" she cried. "You're alive!" She released her father from his tight
hold and ran over to give the older man a hug of his own.

"Oof!" Dr. Waldo grunted, with pleasure, as Eve's forceful hug
knocked the wind out of him. "Yes, yes, yes, I've survived, and
what's more, you have too! Children, I was so worried about you!
Didn't know what we'd done to you, sending you off with that
Dark MATTER, no, shouldn't have done that but didn't have a
choice did we? And here you are, you're all okay, a relief, I tell you,
a relief!" His eyes glistened in the sun.

Eve pulled away from Dr. Waldo. "It's not okay, Dr. Waldo. We
lost Emma in the ghost universe, and this is still the wrong Charlie," she said.

Milo looked at Parallel Charlie, standing there in Charlie's
clothes, looking very much like the Charlie he'd met. "The wrong

Charlie?" he said.

"Yes, parallel Earth, wrong Charlie, haven't had time to explain it all," mumbled Dr. Waldo, assessing the situation, taking notes and making calculations in his mind. "Ghost universe. Very very bad." He looked at Ben. "You found this one, good, well done. Lost the other. Not good. It happens, not to blame. Well, then, we must find Emma, and we must find the other Charlie and return this Charlie. That's all there is to it, get everyone back in their places, that's what we'll do." His brain whirred and clicked.

"And we still have no idea where to find Vik," said Eve, deflated. Her mission was not just not a success; it was a complete failure.

"Dr. Waldo, what happened in the Hub? How did you survive? We thought you were a goner for sure," said Parallel Charlie. "And we can't get into the Hub at all anymore. Totally locked itself up. Is it okay? Rupert's okay?"

Dr. Waldo looked at Parallel Charlie, studying him as though seeing him for the first time, or perhaps as though he couldn't see him at all. "The Hub," he said, "the Hub, yes, the Hub, the key, a new key…" his voice trailed off, lost in thought. He hopped back to the car and into the back seat.

Milo stepped in to help explain. "We haven't been able to get back in to the Hub yet, either," he said. "Dr. Waldo has been off finding what he thinks will be a key to let us in. He just got back, met us at Ed's cabin. We were just on our way to the lighthouse with the new key."

"He's been off where? A key to let us into the Hub?" repeated Eve. "Something other than the wishing rocks?"

"The wishing rocks don't seem to be working anymore," said Milo. "Dr. Waldo isn't sure why, but he has a theory."

Dr. Waldo returned to the group, tucking something into his lab coat pocket. "Yes, a theory, I have a theory, a new key," he said.

"You see, children, when you left, Vik was still inside the Hub with us. We all—all the scientists in the Hub—we all had personalized pigeons, to take us home, to our individual homes. You know the pigeons—devices that will take you from wherever you are to just one place—"

"Yes, the pigeons," said Parallel Charlie. "We are all very familiar with the pigeons!"

Dr. Waldo looked surprised and a bit alarmed. "Tell me you didn't use your pigeons?" he said in a low, worried tone.

"Um, well, we did," said Eve. "Ben used his accidentally, and Charlie and I didn't have much choice once we were in the ghost universe. The Dark MATTER broke after we used it, and we had no idea how to find an elevator. Why, what's wrong with the pigeons? Didn't you give us good ones?"

"Oh, well, nothing, nothing, I suppose, if you didn't get spread out over the universe then they are fine, apparently, or were," Dr. Waldo said. "I've just discovered a flaw in the pigeons, a bug if you will, a ruffled pigeon feather, might have gone wrong but looks like you're all in one piece, each of you, no worries, but before you use those again I might suggest we get you new versions. Updated, yes, can't have you obliterated, wouldn't be good at all."

"Sorry, Dr. Waldo," said Parallel Charlie, relieved in retrospect that he had not been obliterated but trying to get the older man back on track with his story, "I interrupted you. You were telling us what happened in the Hub?"

"Right, indeed, right. Well, yes, you all left with the Dark MAT-TER—I must get a report from you on how that worked, at a later date, must record the findings, wasn't sure it was going to work, to be honest, but we didn't have much choice did we?—and we were there with Vik in the Hub. The Hub has a mind of its own, you see. I don't believe it would have let Vik kill us in there. We don't know for sure, as we all got out of Dodge, as you people say, fast as we could. Each of us scientists has a pigeon of our own, so as fast as you can say 'how do you do' we all activated our emergency pigeons and flew home to Lero. I immediately tried the elevator again but it didn't work right away, took it an hour or so, so I knew not all was lost, but I couldn't get into the Hub. I decided the best course of action would be to come here and gather up Milo, and I assumed we'd all convene here again at some point, right, indeed, and so we have, so we have."

"But we just came from the elevator on Lero," said Eve. "It didn't look like anyone had been there for a long time."

"Yes, yes, true, well, I've had to do some time travel to get everything back in the right order, couldn't say when I was there, maybe I was there in the future, or perhaps you were there in the past, hard to say, didn't stick around for long, hard to say."

Eve knew enough about the rather impossible task of trying to figure out timelines that she didn't pursue it any further. "Dad mentioned a key?" she said. "The wishing rocks don't work anymore?"

"Right, yes, a key. As you say, the wishing rocks don't work anymore, something's gone wrong. I have a hypothesis, yes, an idea, the entry needs to be reset, like a computer sometimes needs to be reset." He held up a small black box. "I believe," he giggled, "I may have the key! I traveled to Australia to get it, oldest one I could find. A cyanobacteria fossil, from a stromatolite, out at the Hamelin Pool Marine Nature Reserve, had to go quite a distance to get this one! This is where more time travel came in, we haven't mapped the Australia lighthouses yet to find the elevators, apologies to Australia, lovely country, must go back there, have you been? The Cape Inscription lighthouse is not an elevator, tried Babbage Island next, I was certain there would be an elevator there, but no, not so. Point Quobba, that's where I found it, lovely red-topped lighthouse with an elevator inside, beauty it is, had to charm my way a bit with the lighthouse keeper! By then I'd used up all sorts of time, wasn't meant to map the elevators while I was there, was I? But I couldn't help myself, couldn't help myself! A little time travel, then, to give myself enough extra hours to go back to pick up the fossil at the nature reserve and get back here on a regular old aer-o-plane by to-day! What a journey! Took me two days! Give me travel by elevators any day. These cyanobacteria, they date back to about 2.5 billion years ago, a full 200 million years before the Great Oxygenation Event, of course. Stromatolites date back to 3.5 billion years ago. I found a stromatolite with a cyanobacteria fossil. Oldest things I could think of. My hypothesis is that this rock, while not as old as this universe, of course, will be sufficient to reboot the door to the Hub, and let us in. Ancient memory. Speaking to the Hub's ancient mind. Taking it back to its factory settings, if you will." He laughed at his own joke, but his demeanor held an undercurrent of concern.

"We were on our way to the lighthouse to try it out," said Milo, "when we came across you all."

"Let's go, then!" said Parallel Charlie. "What are we waiting for?"

The group piled into Ed's truck, squishing the teens in the back with Milo; Dr. Waldo sat up front with Ed.

"Hold on to each other back there," said Ed. "That back seat isn't made for four!"

"We've survived pigeons and Dark MATTER and a ghost universe," said Parallel Charlie. "I think we can survive a mile without seat belts!"

They bumped along the dirt road, Ed driving as slowly as he could to help lessen the impact of the potholes on his passengers in the back, but all of them willing the pickup to move as fast as it safely could.

As they pulled into the parking lot at the lighthouse, they saw two figures on the short flight of steps leading up to the door.

Sitting at the top of the stairs was Charlie, anguish and fear etched on his face and body, holding a limp and lifeless Emma in his arms.

chapter thirteen

The sneeze that caused Emma to lose her grip with Parallel Charlie, combined with the act of watching him and Eve disappear before her eyes, jolted Emma wide awake and out of her ghost-planet-induced stupor.

"NOOOO!" she cried at the empty space where Parallel Charlie and Eve had stood just moments before. "No, come back!" *They can't be gone. They can't be!* But they were.

A few ghosts wandering by turned, slowly, to see what the disruption was. On seeing nothing of interest, they went on with their business, whatever that business might be.

Emma had been talking with her grandfather before Parallel Charlie had pulled her away. She looked around to find him again, but he was gone, a wisp in the wind. Eve's Great Aunt Doethine, however, was still there, watching Emma with her amused, knowing smile.

"They left without you," said Doethine, when Emma's eyes met hers.

"They didn't mean to," said Emma. "I sneezed. I let go." *How could I have let go? I'm such an idiot. I'm here forever. I'm stuck on this planet forever, all because I sneezed.*

"So you did," said Doethine. Her speech, her movements, everything about her was slow and measured, as though time meant nothing to her. Perhaps, thought Emma, it didn't anymore. Once a person is dead, what is time?

"Come sit with me," said Doethine.

Not knowing what else to do, Emma went and sat. Now that she was thinking a little more clearly than before, she studied this ghost next to her more carefully. Doethine was perched on a bench that stood perpendicular to another bench, with a low table between them at the corner. However, Emma now realized, Doethine was not so much sitting on the bench as she was occupying the space above the bench, in the same way that the ghosts didn't so much walk on the ground as glide over it. It was as though they were going through the motions of life as they remembered it, but those motions weren't really necessary. Emma wondered, could these ghosts go through things? Were they solid? Were they even real? Was this whole place merely a figment of her imagination? Was she dreaming—or, worse, was she dead?

"Am I dead?" she asked.

"No." Great Aunt Doethine, like the man at the desk, was succinct. She offered up nothing more, but instead sat, patiently awaiting Emma's questions.

So she wasn't dead … yet. *At least there's that,* Emma thought. "Can you help me get home?" she asked.

Doethine said nothing.

"No?"

No response.

"Yes?"

No response.

Emma kicked her heels against the bench. This was going nowhere. "You're Eve's Great Aunt, right?" she said, not sure what else to say.

Doethine smiled broadly. This question she would answer. "Yes."

Relieved not to be the only one talking anymore, Emma returned Doethine's smile. "You discovered the elevators?"

Doethine nodded. "I did indeed."

"That's cool," said Emma. She studied Doethine, trying to decide if she could see through her or if it was just a trick of the light. That thought prompted another: where did the light here come from, anyway? She couldn't see a sun, but it could be behind the clouds. In the whole time she'd been on the planet, though—how long? Minutes? Days?—the light hadn't changed. It hadn't gotten brighter; it hadn't gotten darker. The steady unchanging light simply existed as a permanent fixture of the planet, like the benches, like Doethine, like eternity.

"Do you know where I can find an elevator here?" said Emma, trying again. "Being here has been really interesting, but I need to get home." She didn't mention that she wouldn't have a clue what to do once in the elevator. She just knew she needed to get away.

"Do you know how to use one, then?" asked Doethine, echoing Emma's thoughts.

"No." Emma sighed. "But do you know where to find one anyway?"

"There is no elevator here you can use," said Doethine.

Something about the way she said the words made Emma wonder if Doethine was playing word games with her. There was no elevator? Or there was no elevator she could use?

"Do you know how I can get home then?"

"You don't like it here?" Doethine smiled.

"That's not an answer," Emma said, half to herself.

"Neither is that," Doethine laughed.

A small breeze lifted Emma's hair away from her neck. Their conversation had the pace of a slow dance, of a lazy summer day: gentle, easy, unhurried. Doethine continued to gaze benevolently on Emma, waiting for more questions they both knew would come. Emma's languor had not yet returned, but she was alert for any signs of the sluggishness.

She tried a new tack. "How did you find the first elevator? Were you looking for it?"

"I wasn't looking for it. It found me. Or rather, it led me to it. I like to think the universes wanted me to find it," said Doethine fondly. "It was time for the elevators to be found."

"Were you an explorer?"

"I was a scientist," said Doethine, "which I suppose is the same thing."

"Why has no one on Earth found the elevators yet?"

"You've found them, haven't you?"

Emma paused. This was true. She and Charlie hadn't been on a quest to find the elevators, but they had, nonetheless, found them.

"Are we the first?"

"Does it matter?"

Emma was strangely unperturbed by the indirect non-answers. Normally this conversation would have driven her crazy, but today it felt more like a trek through Dr. Waldo's Thought maze. A quest, a labyrinth, a pathway leading her where she needed to go. The way was the way.

"Eve told me her mom may have found a new kind of elevator," said Emma, watching Doethine for any reaction. There was none. "Do you know about that?"

"Do I know about the other kinds of elevators, or do I know that Eve's mom found one?"

"Either."

"Yes."

"So there *are* other kinds of elevators?"

"The universes are infinite, Emma. Do you think an elevator would be the only way to get around?"

Emma pondered this. She had not, of course, thought about this before. She had not thought much beyond her own life before. But she supposed, having seen all she'd seen the last few days (weeks? months?), if everything was indeed possible (as seemed more and more likely, or at least, everything was possible *somewhere*), that it was more likely than not that one could travel through the multiverse in a multitude of ways, if one could just figure those ways out.

"Is Eve's mom still alive?"

Doethine nodded slowly. "Eve's mom is still alive."

Emma pursed her lips. She realized she hadn't been specific enough. "I mean, alive in an alive way, not alive in a ghost way like you. No offense. Just, I mean, is she alive in a way she could come home to Eve one day, to Lero?"

Doethine didn't answer.

"Are you not allowed to tell me?" asked Emma.

"It's not time for you to know," said Doethine.

"How do you know?"

"I know." Doethine spoke like a heartbeat in the morning: slow, steady, calm.

Emma felt herself being lulled into a peacefulness again, not as strongly as before, but she was aware she would need to find a way home soon, before it was too late, before she forgot she needed to leave at all. Still, she had more questions.

"You know a lot," she said.

Doethine tilted her head.

Not expecting much of an answer, Emma asked, "Do you know about Vik? About The Void?"

The features on Doethine's serene face grew more serious. "I do," she said.

"Can you tell me about it? Who is The Void? What does it want?"

Doethine was quiet a long time. Emma started to think Doethine was not going to answer, but then the ghost spoke.

"Yes, I think it's time for you to know. The Void," she began, "is as old as time. Some argue over whether The Void is one entity or many; that's the same as arguing whether water is one entity or many. Water is water. If you pour more water into water, you have water. A drop of water away from a bucket of water is still water. The Void is like that.

"Some believe The Void should be destroyed completely. I don't think it's as simple as that. What I believe is that The Void has overstepped its bounds, and that is what must be stopped. It has its place in the multiverse, but now it wants more."

"What does it want?" asked Emma.

"What does any living entity want?" asked Doethine.

Emma considered this. What did any living entity want? How would she know? She was just a teenager. Ghost planets, The Void, all of it was beyond her imagination. What did any living entity want?

To live.

"What?" said Emma.

"I said, 'What does any living entity want?'" said Doethine.

"No, after that," said Emma. "What did you say after that?"

"I said nothing," said Doethine, smiling.

To live. Emma was certain she'd heard it. From where? From whom? "To live?" she said, out loud.

"Exactly," said Doethine. "The most fundamental, basic desire of living entities, at least those with consciousness, is simply to live."

Doethine continued. "Not so long ago, cosmically speaking, The Void lived, quietly, harmlessly, mostly within black holes and other places far from the reach of intelligent life. The Void existed on stardust and emptiness; it sustained itself quite well for a very long time. Most of the time, The Void would sleep, for eons at a time, something like a hibernating bear. However, there came a time when someone, somewhere, discovered the first elevator." She smiled benevolently at Emma, leaned in as if to tell her a secret. "This was long before my time. I was not the first; I was just the first on Lero."

She leaned back, smoothed her dress across her knees. "There has been much debate as well around the elevators, their origin and their purpose. Personally, I believe they, too, are as old as time. I believe the elevators were put there to help us find each other, to connect us.

"The most powerful phrase in all the universes, Emma: 'You are not alone.' And you are not. We are not. None of us is alone. I believe the elevators were put there to help us remember that, to help us know there are always others out there, maybe not exactly like us, but yet still living, struggling, celebrating, loving, hoping, suffering, persevering, like all of us. None of us is ever alone.

"But it doesn't feel that way always, does it? The more advanced a civilization becomes, the more isolated the people often become. People start to become disconnected. They start to compare themselves more against others, judge more, and too often they feel themselves come up short. Some may start to shrink down, live smaller lives, out of fear of judgment, and that only exacerbates the problem.

"And that's where The Void comes in. Once, long ago, when the first elevator was discovered by that first intelligent life form, it opened up more than just the connection between thin spots. Somehow it awakened The Void nearby, and some of The Void, we believe, slipped through.

"Do you remember, Emma, the first time you had chocolate?"

Emma shook her head. "Not really."

Doethine nodded. "Well, I imagine that for The Void, being exposed to intelligent life might have been like what it was for someone on Earth to eat chocolate for the first time. The Void, as you know, can slip into minds and eat. You don't know The Void is there. It got a taste of the chemicals released when a person is disconnected from others, isolated, and I imagine it was like eating candy. It wanted more."

Remembering how Eve had made this same chocolate analogy when they were stuck in the cave on the planet of plassensnares, Emma smiled. She wondered where Eve and Parallel Charlie had ended up. Something inside her thought she remembered Parallel Charlie holding a device—could it have been a pigeon? She wasn't sure. She hoped whatever had happened to them, that they were safe. Safe from whatever might harm them. Safe from plassensnares; safe from The Void.

"Is The Void evil" Emma asked.

"I'm not convinced that The Void is evil," said Doethine. "I rather suspect The Void simply *is*. It exists. It is as indifferent to you as a cold virus is. It doesn't mean to destroy you; it just means to survive. But The Void is now surviving at the expense of intelligent beings like yourself."

"If it doesn't want to hurt people, then why is it? Why won't it stop?" Emma asked.

"It doesn't want to hurt people, nor does it *not* want to hurt people," Doethine said. "The Void just wants *to live.*"

"What happens if it wins? If it takes over a person's mind?"

"If The Void wins," said Doethine, "a society falls apart. Creatures that were meant to live apart are not affected, but intelligent beings such as your people and mine, we need each other. What is your saying, 'No man is an island'? I heard a story once about a young man on your planet who went into the wild to find himself. He ended up dying, tragically, but not before he wrote: 'Happiness is other people.' No, your people and my people, without each other, we wither inside. I have seen the results of a whole planet of people succumbing to The Void. It was not pretty."

"So how do we fight it? What do we do?" asked Emma. "If it's just inside our heads, floating in like air, how do we have a chance against it? Eve said The Void is already on Earth. Do we even have a chance?"

"The Void is so successful because it gets into your head and infiltrates your mind. The Void sounds just like your own inner voices, the ones that tell you you're not good enough as you are, that you should stay home because you aren't good at talking with people, that you shouldn't try anything because you might fail and only successful efforts are worthy. These voices are the same as The Void's. The Void doesn't have to create them; it just perpetuates them.

"It's almost too easy for The Void, with beings such as us. People don't want to admit they're alone, that they're lonely, because it feels like an admission, like proof they don't belong. That it's a badge of dishonor, stating 'I have been rejected. I am not enough.' All The Void has to do is get people disconnected from each other, and then the shame of telling anyone is far too great; the emptiness opens the way for loneliness, and The Void feasts. Few things are as dangerous, Emma, as forces that are able to make us believe we are alone—even if we are not.

"As it is so often, the actions that will save people are the very things they start to shy away from. People start to stay away from other people, stop reaching out for community and friendship, when only being with others will save them. People stop creating art, but art will save them. People turn away from dance, but dance would save them. The things that make people feel vulnerable are the very things that will save them. You are not alone. Sometimes you have to be the one to reach out and let people know that you need them, but you are never alone.

"The Void can't stand creativity, discovery, a sense of adventure. That's why it is trying to destroy the Hub. You've been there. You've seen the fruits of Dr. Waldo's vast imagination. Do you think The Void can thrive there? Of course not. It is now using Vik to try to destroy the Hub, so it can spread freely. The Hub is a road block for The Void, and it wants it gone."

"Is Dr. Waldo okay? Is the Hub okay? Did Vik destroy it?" asked Emma.

Doethine said nothing.

Recognizing that a lack of answer from Doethine did not necessarily mean something bad, Emma took a deep breath and continued. "Okay, so how do we stop The Void" she asked.

"How do you fight it?" said Doethine. "Be compassionate. Be courageous. Connect. You have to dig down past your own fears to empathize with what the other is going through. If you imagine that you could never feel what the other felt, you can never connect with them. Step into their story from their perspective."

Emma waited for Doethine to say more, but the woman was done talking about The Void. Emma absorbed what Eve's Great Aunt had said. How, Emma wondered, could she begin to see things from The Void's perspective, step into its story? Even the thought of it was frightening, to expose herself, her mind, to such vulnerability. Was it the only way? Surely there must be another way to fight. But when she tried to think of one, she came up blank.

The two sat in silence.

"Do I have to stay here?" Emma asked after a while. Even if leaving meant going back where The Void was, she wanted to get home.

"You know the answer to that," Doethine said. "You know the answer to all these questions, you realize." She stood up and started walking, or gliding, slowly. "We've been sitting too long," she said. "I like to walk."

Emma stood and walked along with her.

"I once met a woman from your Earth," Doethine said. "She told me my name, Doethine, reminded her of the name Dorothy. She told me about a girl named Dorothy in a movie that's famous on your planet. About a wizard, a young girl, her dog? They find themselves far from home, somehow, and Dorothy is trying to get back. Do you know it?"

Emma nodded. "Of course. The Wizard of Oz."

"Yes, that's it. The Wizard of Oz. The woman told me that at the end of the movie, Dorothy learns she always had the power to go home, that she had the power all along."

Emma looked down at her own shoes as she walked, subconsciously tapping together the heels of her sneakers. Not ruby slippers, but …

"I have the power in me already?" Emma said.

Doethine said nothing.

"Do you mean I can get home without an elevator?"

Doethine's smile grew. She shrugged her shoulders. "You are stardust, Emma. You are made of the multiverse. You already have everything you need. You've had it all along." The ghost of Great Aunt Doethine paused in her walk; Emma stopped as well. Doethine smiled, kissed Emma on the forehead, and glided away, slowly, without hurry, without a backward look, without another word.

Emma wracked her brain. If she already had everything she needed, what did she have? *Think, Emma, think!* What did she have? What did she even need? Okay, she thought, time to make a list. She reached into her backpack to pull out her notebook, then burrowed to the bottom to find a pen. As her fingers searched around, she touched something hard and round.

"Wait," she said out loud. "Is that …?"

She pulled out the object to see what it was.

"The rock!" she whispered loudly. "The rock from the beach!" She rolled it between her fingers, the rock she'd found days (weeks? months?) ago when she and her own Charlie were roaming on the beach below the lighthouse, the rock like Eve's energy rock. The rock that she'd showed to Charlie, and after he'd held it and given it back to her, she'd thought she'd seen trails of light following him …

"That's it!" she cried out. Emma looked around her to see if her outburst had disturbed anyone on the ghost planet, but apparently the denizens of the ghost planet were more or less imperturbable. She kissed the rock, knowing without question: this rock would lead her back to Charlie. *You are made of the multiverse. You already have everything you need.*

Emma hurried to repack everything into her backpack. She looked around. "Goodbye, ghost planet," she said to no one in particular. No one listened; no one heard. Emma squeezed her eyes shut, wrapped her fingers tightly around Charlie's rock, and with all her mind and all her being imagined Charlie: his laugh, his way of befriending everyone so easily. The way he both ceaselessly teased her and yet was also fiercely protective of her. The way his wavy hair would fall into his eyes when he leaned over his work—whether homework or fixing his bike or anything else—lost in concentration. She thought of the times they'd been up half the night giggling when they were supposed to be in their own rooms sleeping. The times he helped her build houses out of shoeboxes for her dolls. The times he sat and listened to her when she was sad, and then punched her arm when she was done crying. She pictured him on the parallel Earth at the lighthouse, the last time and place she saw him.

"Take me to Charlie," she said to the rock and to the multiverse, and she set her focus on how it felt when the Dark MATTER had brought them here: the everythingness inside herself, the infinity, the being one with all the universes. She let the feeling wash over her again. Starting with the fingers wrapped around the energy rock, Emma's body began to tingle and glow from within. She felt the air squeeze out of her, the choking feeling of being unable to breathe. But then she became the air and the oxygen itself and didn't need to breathe. She felt her whole body vibrating, each cell individually, and she saw herself inside herself, able to count every cell if she'd wanted to. Emma smelled the emptiness of eternity, and knew she had left the ghost planet. She was everywhere. She was the multiverse. With great intensity, Emma brought her focus to the parallel Earth, to Charlie, focused on bringing her body back together, pulling her atoms and molecules away from the everythingness to form Emma again, separate again from the multiverse, apart from but always a part of it.

She opened her eyes.

"What? What the—? What?" mumbled Charlie, scrambling in panic under his covers. Emma was standing next to his bed in his bedroom in the cabin, lit only by the glow of the full moon streaming through the window in the dark of night. The sound of movement in his bedroom had awakened him.

Emma dropped the rock and fell to the floor, weak and drained. Her breathing was shallow; her skin was pale.

"Emma! Emma, are you okay? What happened? How did you get here?" Charlie flashed out of bed, turned on the light, and kneeled next to his sister. "Emma! Is that you? Are you okay?"

His shouts awoke the others in the house. Parallel Amy Renee was the first to come running to the room, followed closely by Parallel Glen and Parallel Emma.

Emma's strength returned quickly. She looked around her at the concerned faces on the clones of the family she loved. And Charlie. Her Charlie. This was the right one. She threw her arms around him and hugged him tightly, as though she were trying to hug him into herself.

"Oh my gosh, Charlie, I can't believe it. I did it. I found you." Emma pulled out of the hug and punched Charlie in the shoulder. "Do not ever, ever, *ever* do something like that again! I might have lost you forever!" She started crying and collapsed into Charlie's chest.

An enormous smile broke out on Charlie's face. "It's you! It's my Emma!" He wrapped her in a hug again, swaying as he held her, tears threatening to overflow his green eyes.

"What is going on?" said Parallel Amy Renee. "Emma, how did you get back here? Where is everyone else?"

Emma explained in great brevity, leaving out all but the most important facts. The family would have questions, she knew, but she would have to leave them unsatisfied.

"A ghost universe?" said Charlie, when she'd finished. "And you got here *on your own?* But ..."

"I know, I know," said Emma. "There's no time to explain. I don't know what's happened to the others but we have to get back to Earth—our Earth—and see if we can find everyone. With the elevators not working, and I don't even know what happened to Dr. Waldo and the Hub ... we need to get back, Charlie. And we need to find the other Charlie, and bring him home."

Emma looked at her parallel family, at her parallel self. She envied Charlie the chance to get to know these people and spend time here. She was sad to leave again so quickly. *Maybe I can come back one day,* she thought, but she didn't have much hope.

"Thank you for taking care of Charlie for me," she said. "Last

I saw your Charlie, he was in perfect health, don't worry. We will find him and get him back to you, I promise." As the words fell out of her mouth, Emma knew she was making an enormous promise that she had no right to make, and no idea how she would keep. Still, hearing the words aloud gave her resolve. She would find this family's Charlie, and she would return him to his home.

The goodbyes were different from regular goodbyes. These were goodbyes filled with longing and wonder and no small amount of confusion. They'd all gotten to more or less the same point in their lives: a family of four, a cabin, an island. Would their lives continue on the same path or would they diverge? Their parting was weighed down by the fullness of knowing they might never know.

"All right," said Emma to Charlie, when they were ready to leave, "hold my hand. Hold it tight. I don't know if this will work again."

"You don't … but maybe we should try the elevator?" Charlie could see that Emma had, in fact, managed to travel through space and time herself, but he was skeptical as to whether he wanted to risk his own molecules.

"Do you know how to operate the elevator?" Emma said. "If it's even working, that is."

Charlie let out a heavy sigh. "I guess not. Beam us out, Emmy. And if you're about to kill us, please make it quick and painless." Resolved to whatever would come next, if anything, he closed his eyes, holding Emma's left hand with both of his.

"I'm not going to kill us," said Emma. *I hope,* she thought.

Emma narrowed her focus to one thing: home. For a fleeting moment her imagination took her back to her family's house, but she shifted the image in her mind to hone in again on Dogwinkle Island—this time, on her own planet Earth. She thought of her mother, her father; she thought of the camping spot where she and Charlie had scanned the skies for UFOs or northern lights—hoping for the latter, never in a million years expecting the former. She took her mind back to the lighthouse, the trail down to the beach where she'd found the energy rock that was now tucked safely in her backpack. She imagined the pictures on the walls, the ones where Eve appeared over and over again, through time. She thought of the storage closet, of discovering the Hub for the first time. She focused her mind and body and being on holding tight to Charlie, on making sure he was as much a part of her as her own limbs, and then she put forth her request to the multiverse: *Take us back where we belong. Take us back to the lighthouse at Balky Point, on our own dear planet Earth, our own world, our own home.*

Their bodies glowed from the inside out, hummed in time with the secret pulse of the universes. They felt the air sucked out of them, then felt their bodies infused with the lightness of infinity. From within the everythingness, Emma sought and found her target: the lighthouse on their Earth.

But something got in the way.

Suddenly, as Emma was concentrating, she felt the emptiness rush in with a great force. "Charlie!" she yelled out; whether in her mind or with some actual voice, she had no idea. "Charlie, hang on!" She could no longer feel his hand, much less anything physical; she was just mind and molecules and space. Vast, open space. She felt herself reassembling into a being again, but falling, tumbling, through the universes, lost …

Thump!

She hit ground, hard, landing face down, like a belly flop.

"Ouch," said a voice next to her.

"Charlie!" mumbled Emma into the dirt, a statement of relief. He was here with her … wherever "here" was.

"You're bleeding," said Charlie from her side.

With great effort, Emma pushed herself up from the ground and into a sitting position, her body radiating pain to her core. Her chest felt as though she had been hit with, well, a planet. A planet that got in the way of their getting home.

She looked around. They could have been on Earth, almost, in a dry, hard desert, somewhere, but somehow she knew they weren't. A look at the sky confirmed this: two suns. Emma squinted, wiped her eyes.

"Where are we?" she asked.

Charlie gave her a small smile. "I was really hoping you'd know that, Em."

Emma felt a wave of anger at herself for having brought them to this place. *How arrogant,* she thought, *how arrogant of me to believe I had a clue what I was doing!*

"I'm so sorry," she said to her brother.

He pulled up his sleeve to cover his hand, and brought the cloth to Emma's forehead. He gently dabbed at the blood trickling from a small wound. "Forgot my first aid kit," he said, with a dry laugh.

Emma pushed his hand away and stood up. Immediately her legs buckled under her, and she fell back to the ground.

"Maybe I should have waited a bit before trying this again," she said, ruefully.

Charlie just nodded. "Well," he said. "So, now what?"

Emma was exhausted. For a moment she begrudged her brother the restful time he'd had down on the parallel Earth—no dinosaur planet, no ghost planet, no Vik ...

"Vik," she said. The thought hadn't occurred to her before, but saying it, she knew: somehow, they were here because of Vik.

And, sure enough, as though he'd been waiting for her cue, a man came walking toward them from the distance. The two suns made the air shimmer. *Just like in a western,* thought Emma as the figure grew nearer, *except I'm defenseless.*

Charlie looked from Emma to the man and back. "It's Vik?" he asked.

The young man with the jet-black hair was dressed all in black, dark like the night, just like in the picture Eve had showed them what seemed like ages ago.

He stopped in front of them. "It's Vik," the man said. "Emma and I have met. So glad you came here. Saved me a trip."

Emma stared him directly in the eyes. She could see a conflict in his face, as though he was of two minds. Quickly, one of those minds took control. His look hardened.

"Why are we here?" Emma demanded. She struggled to breathe regularly. Regardless of whether the air on this planet was breathable or the amber rock on her bracelet was protecting her, Emma's lungs felt as though they could never get enough air again. She tried to hide her efforts, but Vik saw.

"Don't worry, you'll be back to normal soon enough. Until, I suppose, we get rid of you. Small detail."

Charlie turned his head at Vik's choice of pronoun. "We? Who is we? What do you want with Emma?" He looked around, but saw no one else.

"Vik," said Emma, "and The Void." Her eyes never left Vik's.

"Vik and The Void," said Vik. "Very good! Clever one, you are. But," he went on, tossing his hands in the air, "that won't help you. You made a very big mistake, young lady. Learning to travel like that, without the elevators. Shouldn't have done that. Now everyone will want to, and we can't have that."

The suns were beating down on this dusty planet. *It's so hot,* thought Emma. *So hot, just like …*

"Wait," she said. "I've been here before." The dry planet where she'd landed with Eve, Ben, and Parallel Charlie, just before they'd ended up on the planet with the plassensnares. This was the same planet. The realization came to her, quick and certain. Those thoughts she'd had, the thoughts that told her the others would never notice if she stayed there without her, had that been …?

"Clever! Clever indeed! You *have* been here before," said Vik. "You're right, we were with you, in your mind. We almost got you that time."

"Doethine told me about you," said Emma, "and Eve told me, too. I know all about you." *I am not alone. I am not alone.* Emma chanted the words in her mind, trying desperately to keep The Void from infiltrating again.

Vik sneered. "You know nothing. They know nothing, and you know nothing. And Eve, Doethine, where are they now? What good are they to you? You *are* alone. You're alone here. Alone in the multiverse, and all you have is this one." He looked at Charlie and sneered. "We'll do away with him quickly enough. Give up, Emma, before I have to hurt you both."

Charlie stood there, helpless and bewildered. Emma hadn't gotten to the point of telling him about Doethine, or Vik, or any of this. He had no idea what they were facing.

But Emma did.

"I'm not alone," Emma said, reaching for Charlie's hand. He grasped it and held tight. "I'm never alone."

"Oh, sure," said Vik, "twins, always have someone there with you, do you? Where was Charlie when you were on the ghost planet? No one but you. Even your grandfather walked away from you. And why wouldn't he? What do you have to offer, Emma? And Eve and the other Charlie, they left you all by yourself to die. Really, what do you matter?"

Emma flinched. It was true, her grandfather had walked away, but that was the ghost planet. Things were different there. And they'd already talked. And Eve and the other Charlie's leaving without her wasn't their fault. She had sneezed.

Vik went on. "And even if you are a twin, that means nothing. You're still separate people. You still get lonely. You know I'm right." Vik paused, got a thoughtful look on his face, as though he was listening. "Charlie leaves you sometimes, doesn't he? He goes off all the time without you. Oh, I know, you think he's your protector, but you know better, deep down you know he's only there for you because he feels he has to be." Vik's false empathy dripped from his words. "He's more of a social butterfly, isn't he? Goes to parties without you sometimes? You'd like to be out, too, out having fun with the other kids? Out with Ben, maybe? Ben, who so clearly prefers Eve, who's not even human. That must sting, Emma. Don't you want to get away from all that pain? It's easy, you know. You can just stay here, stay with us."

Emma gripped her brother's hand tighter. "Don't listen to him, Charlie. He just wants to get into our minds. Don't let him get to you."

"Don't worry about Charlie, Emma," said Vik. "Charlie is the life of the party! Charlie always comes through just fine. But you, you've felt it, haven't you? That fear, knowing you're not good enough for those other kids. You let them see the real you once, a couple times, didn't you, and now you know you've revealed too much. Now they know you for who you are. They know you're a fraud, Emma. They know you don't belong. They know you're not one of them. You never could be, never will be. You're outside. You'll always be outside. Don't be sad. It's easier to be alone, if you just give in to it. Stop trying to fit in, Emma. Because you know you never will, don't you? Nothing you do will ever be good enough. Nothing you say. Who you are, Emma, is just not enough."

Emma's breathing was shallow again, not from the impact of falling on the planet, but from the humiliation and shame. She knew what he was saying was true. Her eyes started to fill up with tears. All the times she was home alone, wanting to be part of a group, wanting to be included, wanting some proof that she was somehow wanted. She felt the pain of it filling her chest, as real as if it were happening again. The voices in her head started chanting loudly. *You're not good enough. You'll never fit in. You don't belong.*

At her side, Charlie felt Emma slipping away from him. He didn't understand what was happening, but he knew Vik's words were affecting his sister. "Don't listen to him, Emma. You know people love you. You're just quieter. I'm more of an extrovert. But you have friends. You have me. You are not alone."

You are not alone. Charlie's words rang in Emma's head. *You are not alone.* What had Doethine told her? The most powerful words in the multiverse. *The things that make people feel vulnerable are the very things that will save them. You are not alone. Sometimes you have to be the one to reach out and let people know that you need them, but you are never alone …*

"Charlie, help me!" said Emma, grabbing both his hands. "Think of Eve, and Ben, and Dr. Waldo, and Milo. And the other Charlie! Bring him too. Help me bring them here!"

"Bring them here? What do you mean? I don't know how!"

"Just think of them! Think of them as hard as you can! Imagine them here with us!" Emma imagined Eve, and Ben, and Dr. Waldo, and Milo, and Parallel Charlie. She imagined them as hard as she could, imagined them entering the emptiness and having their breath taken away only to be replaced by being a part of the every-thingness. She imagined them glowing from within and dispersing into infinity, and then with all her might she imagined them reassembling here, on this dry, dusty planet, wherever "here" might be. "Please," she whispered to the universes. "Please, I need them."

She opened her eyes.

There, looking rather bewildered, standing before them, were Eve, Ben, Dr. Waldo, Milo, and Parallel Charlie. And Ed.

"Ed!" she said. "You too?"

"Charlie told me to come!" He held up his phone and some portable speakers. "He said to bring these?"

Emma looked at the phone and the speakers, puzzled, then burst into a smile. "Yes! Charlie told you to bring those? Charlie, you're brilliant! Turn on some music, Ed! We are having ourselves a dance."

"We are what?" said Ben.

"We are dancing," said Emma.

"We are what?" echoed Parallel Charlie.

A peppy song poured out from Ed's speakers. "Glad I charged this thing earlier," he joked nervously, "Didn't know I'd be bringing it on a trip!"

"Trust me!" said Emma firmly to the gathered crowd, who remained standing quite still. "Just *dance!*"

Eve, quickly understanding the situation and Emma's intentions, grabbed both Charlies, one by each hand, and led them in a jumping, swaying, arm-waving, bouncing sort of dance. Milo reached out to Ed and spun him into a gregarious swing dance. Dr. Waldo, ever a jig man, danced his own joyful jig.

Emma looked at Ben and held out her hand. "Dance with me?" she said. Her heart fluttered as she said it, but she didn't look away from his dark eyes.

"But ..." Ben protested. "I don't dance."

"Don't be ridiculous. You may not dance *well*," she said, "but that doesn't matter, so long as you're dancing." She placed her hands on his shoulders, and Ben automatically responded by putting his hands around her waist. They swayed in time with the music, their moves more awkward than award-winning, but both were smiling. Emma's heart surged with joy. She could feel her brain unclouding;

The Void, she knew, was making its escape. Her smile grew.

Before too long, everyone was lost in the joy of movement, their inhibitions left behind. When Emma turned her head to put it on Ben's shoulder, she saw Vik, standing off to the side, alone.

"Ben," she said, "keep dancing. I need to ..." She released herself from his hold and walked over to Vik.

"Vik," she said, "may I have this dance?"

A struggle washed over Vik's face. Again Emma could see two minds working behind his eyes, and this time she knew: one was Vik; the other was The Void.

Rather than wait to see which mind would win Emma reached out and placed Vik's right hand on her waist, then held his left hand with her right. In ninth grade gym class students had had an option of taking a quarter of dance or a quarter of kickboxing. Emma had wanted to take kickboxing, but had psyched herself out of it, thinking she couldn't handle the intensity. Ever since then she'd regretted her choice, but today she was glad for it. She led Vik in a gentle waltz, counting out the steps for him and completely ignoring his weakening sounds of protest.

Be compassionate. Emma heard Doethine's words repeating in her head. *Step into their story from their perspective.*

"I heard about your friend dying," said Emma. "I'm so sorry. I can't even imagine how much that would hurt. That must have been horrible." Emma felt the tiniest bit of tension flow out of Vik's hold.

"... Thank you," said Vik haltingly. "It was."

As quickly as Vik had loosened his grip, it rushed back in again, The Void reclaiming its hold on him. Vik stiffened, and Emma struggled to keep him in her hold.

"It was his fault," said Vik. "I don't need friends, anyway. My life is better without other people. Other people just make trouble.

They're only concerned with their own lives. They say they care about you, and then they ignore you. Other people are unreliable and only cause pain. I am happiest when I am alone."

"That can't be true," said Emma, pulling Vik with her as she stepped back and to the side in three-quarter time. "Sure, relationships are challenging, but they're worth it. You were right, earlier, when you said I often wish I were out at the parties, too. Being around people is sometimes scary for me, because I don't always know the right thing to say. I feel like an idiot. But at the same time, my favorite times are times I've spent with friends."

The words tumbled out of Emma, but she could tell she wasn't having any effect on Vik. *Keep trying,* she told herself, though she felt ready to give up. *Be courageous.*

"What do you like to do?" she asked, scrambling for a connection. "Like, do you like dancing? Or, do you like to build things? When I was a kid, on our planet we had these little brick building blocks, and Charlie and I loved to make houses. I never really played with dolls, but I loved to build houses for them. Did you ever do anything like that?"

For a fleeting moment, Vik—the real Vik—was back again. "I always liked building bridges," he said. "I liked to see how much weight I could get them to hold."

Was that a smile? Not really, Emma decided, but it was the beginning of one. "That's awesome!" she said. "Bridges are amazing. The fact that people can build something over water, without any supports in the middle, that's sort of incredible, isn't it?"

"Bridges are unnecessary," said The Void through Vik. "Connection is unnecessary. People have what they need, where they are."

Without realizing it, Emma had led Vik away from the rest of the group, farther away than she cared to be. Holding her fear in check, she gently guided their dance in an arc until they were turned around, and started leading them back to the others.

"Connection is absolutely necessary," she said. "No one person can provide everything for himself. We need each other. You had the right idea when you built those bridges. And besides, building them was fun, wasn't it?"

Vik looked at her. "It was." He looked away as The Void tried another tactic. "Look, your friends, they've forgotten you again already. They aren't even paying attention to you."

Emma didn't bite. "No, you're wrong. They're watching. They trust me. They know I'm strong, and so do I. And if I need them, they're right there for me."

"They didn't come with you."

"They would have if I'd asked."

Vik and The Void were silent. Emma took the opportunity to try again.

"Vik," she said, "isn't it hard on you, living with all this anger and pain inside you? This dancing, this is nice, isn't it? Being with people again instead of being all alone? I know it's scary. It's scary for me sometimes, too. It's scary for me right now. A lot scary. But it's nice, right?"

Emma kept her eyes on his, refusing to look away. She would not abandon the young man inside. She would stay with him as she knew her friends would do for her. *Step into their story from their perspective.* "I can't imagine how awful it would be to lose a friend. The grief. The feeling that no one else could understand. And The Void, it slipped right in. But The Void lied to you, Vik. People do understand. And even if they don't, they're here to listen. I'm here to listen. Dr. Waldo, he knows people who can help you. People who can give you your life back—a real life, not this shell of a life. You have to want it, though, Vik. You have to believe it's worth it. You have to decide you are willing to fight for it. It has to start with you."

Vik's eyes filled with tears. The struggle within him played out like a light switch going on and off, on and off, on and off. In his eyes, Emma could see him fighting, knew there was hope, but also knew she couldn't help him by herself. She had to do something, and she had to do something now.

Doethine, help me, she thought. *I don't know if I can manage what I'm about to try. Help me.*

With all the energy Emma had left in her, she gathered up her friends in her mind for one last trip, and took everyone home.

chapter fourteen

Charlie sat on the steps of the lighthouse, on the verge of tears as he held Emma, not knowing what to do. Last he knew, he'd been dancing with Eve and the other Charlie on some desolate planet; then, suddenly, he was here. He'd felt dizzy and discombobulated on arrival back on Earth, so it took him a few minutes to realize Emma was in a far worse condition. Her face was ashen, she was barely breathing, and her heartbeat was more of a puff than a pulse. He'd carried her outside, for fresh air and hoping to find the others there—where had they gone? Had Emma not brought them back, too?—and it was there he was sitting when Ed and the others drove up in Ed's truck.

"You're back! Guys, I don't know what happened to Emma. Something went wrong when she brought us all back here. I think she's traveled through the universes too many times. This last one was too much, bringing all of us home. Someone, help her! Dr. Waldo, can you help?" Charlie pleaded without stopping for breath.

"What are you saying?" said Dr. Waldo, rushing to Emma's side, feeling her forehead. It was cold and clammy. "She's traveled through the universes? What do you mean?"

"And what do you mean, 'brought all of us back here'?" said Milo. Emma's eyes fluttered.

"Emma are you there?" said Dr. Waldo. He checked her pulse. "I'm not a medical doctor," he said, flustered. "I don't ... if we could just get in the Hub ..."

"Charlie, what do you mean 'brought all of us back here'?" Milo repeated.

Charlie looked at him, confused. "What do I mean? Don't you know?" Then, realization spread over his face. "Do you mean you haven't gone yet? It's time, isn't it, time travel, you told us it's tricky, it must still be in your future, Emma got us back before you left ... Emma, you brilliant little dork, how did you do that?" Charlie stopped talking out loud, but his lips still moved, talking to himself as he worked through the sequence of events. After a few moments, he looked up and spoke again. "Ed!" he said. "Ed, do you have a phone and speakers?"

Puzzled by this odd change of topic, Ed hesitated. "I guess I do, in the car? But Emma—"

"Go get your phone and your speakers, and hang on to them ... and hang on tight to Dr. Waldo, Emma doesn't know she's bringing you too ..."

Ed stared at Milo. "Charlie, are you okay? She doesn't know she's bringing me where? You're not making any sense."

Charlie grew red in the face. "GET THE SPEAKERS!" he yelled. "Get them, and then hang on to Dr. Waldo, I just know it works, but I don't know when ..."

Shaking his head, Ed jogged to his car, got his phone and portable speakers out of the glove compartment, and came back to stand next to Dr. Waldo. He linked elbows with with the gray-haired scientist and held tight.

"Milo!" said Charlie. "Get Ed's other arm. I don't know ... I mean I know she did it, but ..."

Milo, more familiar with things that made no sense, asked no questions. He stood at Ed's other side and wrapped his arm around Ed's, while Ed struggled to hang on to the phone and speakers at the same time.

"I don't know when it's going to happen, but just be ready," said Charlie. "Ben, Charlie, Eve, you too, you're all going, too. Will you all go? We need you! You have to go!"

"Of course, whatever you need," said Eve. "But Charlie, where are we—"

And then they were gone.

Breathing heavily, Charlie stared at the empty spaces where the six people had been just moments before. "She got them all. She got them all." He looked down at Emma, still in his arms. "You got them all, Emma, I mean, I knew you did, because I was there, but you got them all, good job." He kissed her forehead. "Good job, Emma. Now, I guess, bring them back when you're ready, which you already did, except where are the rest of them?" He rambled on in his state of panic.

The familiar sound of Charlie's voice seeped through Emma's mind, tickling her brain cells and waking them up. Her eyelids fluttered again, and this time she opened her eyes.

"Charlie?" she said in a hoarse whisper. "Is that you? The real you? Where are we?"

Charlie wept with relief as Emma raised herself up to a sitting position. She sat next to her brother and leaned heavily on him for support, looking around.

"Are we back on Earth? Our Earth? Back at the lighthouse?"

"Yes, it's me! Yes, we are," said Charlie. "You did it, Em, you got us home." He held her tight, put his chin on the top of her head. "Emma. My Em. You're going to be okay."

"What's wrong?" she said, sensing there was something Charlie wasn't telling her.

"The others," said Charlie. "I don't know where they are. You got us—you and me—back here before the rest of them had left. Now they're off on that planet, I guess, but I don't know if you got them back, or where they are."

Emma took in this information. She was sapped, tired to her bones. She could not imagine being more weary and still being alive. Traveling on her own accord through the universes, three times, bringing people along with her, pulling them out of their own worlds to come to hers, had taken an immense toll on her. She knew without a doubt that she had stretched the boundaries of the rules of the universes.

"Oh, Charlie," she said, shaking her head, "I think I've messed up. I brought all those people to us, and I didn't get permission. That can't be allowed. You can't just pick people up and move them, that has to be against the rules. Maybe that's why they're not back. Maybe I just messed it all up too badly."

"Emma, no!" said Charlie, leaning back to look his sister in the eyes. "I asked them. You got us here before you took them to the other planet … I mean … well, when we got here they were still here and hadn't gone yet, and I asked them if they'd go. Right after I asked, that's when they disappeared."

"They did? You did?" Emma said with relief. "So I didn't take them without their knowing?"

"Well," said Charlie, "I didn't exactly have time to explain everything, but I told them we needed them. Eve said they'd go, and they were gone."

Emma dropped her head back to Charlie's shoulder. "I've missed you, Charlie," she said.

"I missed you, too, Em," he said. "You never did finish telling me where all you went. A ghost universe, and a dinosaur planet, you said? I want to hear all of it."

And so she told him everything.

Emma had finished sharing her stories, and she and Charlie were still sitting on the lighthouse steps, resting, when the others returned. They appeared slowly, a shimmer in the air at first, then growing more solid from moment to moment until finally, they were all reassembled and whole again, back on solid ground.

The returning space travelers looked at each other, stunned.

"How …?" said Ben.

"Emma, did you do that?" said Dr. Waldo. "Did you … travel, without the elevators, without a pigeon, without Dark MATTER? That was dangerous, my child, so very dangerous, do you know?" He looked deeply concerned, but at the same time, he was overflowing with eager questions.

Emma nodded. "I did that," she said with a small smile, still tired, but pleased with herself.

"But how? How did you do that? We've speculated that it's possible, but …"

"Doethine," said Emma, looking at Eve. "Great Aunt Doethine told me how."

"She did?" said Dr. Waldo, incredulous.

"Well, not really. She did and she didn't." Emma took a page from Doethine's book and said no more.

"The time travel, though?" said Ben. "Dr. Waldo, how did she do that? Getting us back at different times? Were we there, and here, at the same time? I don't understand. How is that possible?"

Dr. Waldo shrugged. "Time is tricky, my son. Time is tricky. We were probably not in two places at once, we just weren't all in the same places at the same time," he said, clarifying nothing. "Best not to try too hard to understand. If it happened, then it happened. Sometimes that's all we know. And sometimes, we're not even sure of that."

Of all the travelers, Ed had been the least prepared. "What the heck just happened?" he asked. "One minute Charlie's asking me if I have portable speakers, next minute I'm on some planet with two suns, dancing with Milo like it's the most important thing in the universe, and then I'm back here again. Can someone maybe please explain?" He leaned against the hood of his car and shook his head in disbelief.

"Universes," said Charlie. "Plural."

Milo walked over to Ed, joined him in leaning against the car, put an arm around Ed's shoulders, and started to interpret the chain of events, as best he could.

Watching this, and seeing the people around her, her new friends, Ben, her brother and her parallel brother from another planet, all united in their confused triumph, left Emma feeling a warm glow of satisfaction. She was exhausted, beyond tired, but she was proud of herself. She'd tackled the universes, she'd taken on Vik—

"Vik!" she blurted out, sitting up. "Did he go back to Lero? How can we find out?"

"To Lero? Vik? How would he get there?" Dr. Waldo asked cautiously. "Did you …?"

"That's where I sent him," said Emma, "or at least, that's where I meant to send him. He's still inside his mind, Vik is; The Void hasn't taken him over completely. But I couldn't do everything myself—keep everyone safe, get us all back here, and save Vik. I sent him back to Lero. Is there a way we can find out if he got there? Is the elevator working yet?"

"The elevator!" said Dr. Waldo. "I completely forgot why we were on our way here, before we got … well, sidetracked. Emma, my dear, I have traveled far, yes quite far, far and wide into the depths of Western Australia here on your planet, looking, my dear, looking for the oldest thing I could think of, and I've brought back with me what I believe will be a new key to the Hub. Would you do the honor of joining me to see if it works?"

With a beaming smile, Emma nodded.

Dr. Waldo gleefully quick-stepped through the lighthouse lobby to the storage room, with Emma by his side, held protectively by Charlie as he helped her walk. The others followed closely behind. Dr. Waldo opened the storage room door with his wishing rock. As he switched on the light in the tiny room, everyone piled in, making for a very tight space. Once all limbs were inside, the door closed behind them.

"The moment of truth," said Dr. Waldo, taking a small black box out of his lab coat pocket. He held it out in the palm of his hand. "Emma, would you …?"

The box looked like it might hold an engagement ring or a diamond pendant. Still, Emma knew that if indeed this rock could unlock the Hub again, its worth was far greater than any gemstone. She took the box from Dr. Waldo's hands and opened the lid.

The rock inside had been hewn in two. Wavy lines of black, gray, white, and myriad shades of brown danced over the surface exposed by the cut. Another person might have dismissed this as just a pretty rock, but Emma held it as though it were gold. With the rock clutched tightly in her fingers, she waved her hand in front of the door to the Hub. *Open, dear Hub, we need you back,* she thought.

The doors slid open without hesitation.

Emma gasped. Dr. Waldo gasped.

What they saw before them … was nothing.

A vast, empty space, filled with nothingness.

"All gone," said Dr. Waldo with a deep sigh. "All gone. Back to the beginning."

Emma was ready to console Dr. Waldo when suddenly he hopped

and skipped out of the elevator and into the nothingness.

"Wait, no, don't—" she said, but she stopped mid-sentence when she saw Dr. Waldo standing there in the space, suspended in air as though there were a floor beneath him, holding him up. Even as she watched, a floor started to appear under him, spreading out from beneath his feet. Dr. Waldo stood with a look of great concentration, his gaze fixed on his shoes and the space beyond and around them. The ground he apparently was creating out of nothingness grew wider and bigger, a copy of the short-cropped grassy area that had been there before. Except this time, the grass was blue.

"I get to start all over!" said Dr. Waldo, spreading his arms with joy. "Start from scratch! Thank you, Hub! Everything is possible, you know, everything, now that I know more, know better, I can start all over. Don't you worry, my friends, just a hiccup in the multiverse. The Hub can be taken down, but as long as we are living and breathing with a will to discover, it cannot be destroyed. Come in, come in, come in to the new Hub!"

Emma, the Charlies, and all the rest passed through the doorway onto the newly formed blue grass, mouths gaping in awe.

"Dr. Waldo, are you sure you're up to this? Maybe it's time for someone else to take over?" said Milo.

"Don't be silly," said Dr. Waldo. "I built it the first time, I can build it again! Yes, the Experimental Building had some flaws, you know it did, this time I'll build it better, can't see why not, no need to make it exactly the same, I'll make it better. Maybe some of you have ideas for new rooms?" He looked directly at Emma.

"I will think about it," she said, her heart full of joy. She did have some ideas, indeed.

Three days later, Emma and both Charlies headed back to the light-house. Worried what might happen to Emma if she tried sending Parallel Charlie back herself, using her new-found powers, Dr. Waldo had suggested that perhaps the young man might stay with the Nelsons for a few days, long enough to give Dr. Waldo time to figure out just exactly where in the multiverse Parallel Charlie belonged. Emma had quickly agreed. Exciting adventures aside, getting swept onto a desert planet by a powerful ancient force had been unsettling, to say the least. Emma was interested in learning more about how she might travel again, and Charlie was begging to learn as well, but for now, Emma wanted nothing of travel beyond this little island on her own Earth.

Dr. Waldo had called earlier that afternoon to tell them to come over.

Emma had answered her phone warily, seeing an unusually long number and "The Hub" listed on Caller ID.

"Um, hello?" she had said, not sure who could be on the other end of the line. *No way this call could really be from the Hub!*, she had thought.

Much to her surprise, though, a familiar voice had come through loud and clear. "Emma! Emma it works! I tell you, starting over here in the Hub has been just a delight! This is Dr. Waldo, Emma, my child, and I've found a way to connect into your cellular phone system! It worked! It worked!" Emma had heard Dr. Waldo shouting out to unseen colleagues: "It worked, my friends! It worked!"

"Dr. Waldo, are you in the Hub?" she had asked.

"I am in the Hub, Emma! I am in the Hub, calling you from my new Hub phone! It works anywhere in the multiverse! Well, that is, I should say, it works for calls to both Lero and Earth. Your Earth. Beyond that, we have not yet completed testing. Small sample size, I suppose. Say, now, I meant to tell you, Vik is getting help back at Lero, you saved him, young lady, he sends his thanks, that he does. His family too. They have come to visit him and to get to know him again. It's tough going, you can imagine, certainly, yes, but they are grateful and asked me to tell you they are grateful, and so I tell you, they are grateful. Now that aside, I have figured out the coordinates of the other Charlie's Earth, and I believe, I do believe we are ready to send him back. Would you three come over as soon as you can, please? Say your goodbyes—that is, the other Charlie should say his goodbyes—you'll be staying here—bring the young man here, all of you, come when you can."

"All right. We'll be right there."

As the trio drove to the lighthouse, Emma hoped this would not be their last visit to the Hub. With Vik back at Lero, working with specialists to help him recover and reconnect, Emma wasn't sure there was a need for her and Charlie anymore. Her heart dropped every time she thought about it. What's more, would she see Eve or Milo again? Their mission was done. Would they return to their regular lives back home?

The three drove along in silence, each lost in his or her own thoughts until they reached the lighthouse.

"Charlie, you handsome devil, it's been great getting to know you," Charlie said to Parallel Charlie, as they made their way into the lobby. "You're my kind of guy." He slapped his parallel self on the back.

Parallel Charlie returned the slap. "For some reason, I can't help but like you, too, Charlie. You're an upstanding citizen, a paragon of virtue, an exemplary example of a human being."

Emma rolled her eyes.

"Emma," said Parallel Charlie. "Seriously, what do I say? It was quite a ride. I'm glad we met. You're a pretty special person."

She blushed, and punched him in the shoulder. "Be nice to your sister," she said, softly. "I'll bet she's pretty special too." Even though she'd always have her own Charlie—she hoped—she would miss

Parallel Charlie.

Parallel Charlie nodded and gave his would-be sister a hug.

The group entered the storage room. As soon as the door behind them closed, the door to the Hub opened. Dr. Waldo had been watching and waiting for them on the newly created security cameras.

Emma and the Charlies stepped out onto the blue grass, and looked around them in amazement.

"My, my! Look what you've done to the place!" said Charlie. "Dr. Waldo, you work fast!"

The remodel was by no means complete, but Dr. Waldo had brought in a few fellow scientists who, under his direction, had helped him start to rebuild. Immediately in front of the entrance Dr. Waldo had first and foremost reconstructed the science lab area so he and his colleagues could get back to work. Off in the distance stood the cabins where Milo and Eve had lived. And to the left of the lab area, on a small patch of ground, stood a two-dimensional elephant, quietly picking at fragrant fruit from a tall three-dimensional tree.

"Rupert!" cried Charlie, a huge grin spreading ear to ear. "You brought back Rupert!"

"One can never forget the elephant in the room!" said Dr. Waldo with delight. "My dear friend Rupert, great company, could not have a Hub without him. The rest," he said, looking around at the emptiness, the space where his Experimental Building had been, everything that was now gone, "the rest will come with time. I can't begin to remember everything I had put into the building. Thought, of course, and the Secret Garden, which will probably start planting itself the moment I have it ready again, but beyond that, I just can't remember much. I shall simply have to start from scratch." He lifted his arms to the sky. "Start from Scratch! I hadn't thought of that one before! A Start from Scratch room in the Experimental Building, what would that be, what would that be ..."

Ask me to help you rebuild, thought Emma, *please ask me.* "Do you have a map of the building as it used to exist?" she asked the scientist.

Dr. Waldo nodded solemnly. "That, dear Emma, would have been a very good idea."

The door behind them opened again, and Eve, Milo, and Ben entered the Hub.

"You called?" said Ben, laughing. He saw Emma and gave her a special smile.

"Can you believe it?" said Emma. "Everything he has to do and he starts by figuring out how to call us." She turned to Dr. Waldo. "You're going to miss us, you know."

"Why?" said Dr. Waldo, a sparkle in his eye. "Why would I miss you? Are you going somewhere?"

Emma stared at him, absorbing the implications.

"What about you guys," said Ben to Eve. "Going home?"

The young woman with the impossibly blonde hair shook her head. "I guess you could say we got a little hooked on adventure. There's more to be done. Besides," she added quietly, looking at her father, "we're still looking for my mom."

"You're looking for your mom?" said Charlie.

Emma nudged him quietly and said, "I'll explain later."

Parallel Charlie hugged everyone, giving Emma another extra long hug, said his goodbyes, and walked back into the elevator. Before closing the Hub door behind him, Dr. Waldo handed Parallel Charlie a phone.

"I've put the Hub on speed dial," said Dr. Waldo. "Call when you get there." With a nod and a wink, he closed the door. He entered coordinates into the panel on the Hub side of the elevator, and sent

Parallel Charlie on his way.

The group waited in silence. This was new. How long would it take to confirm travel across universes?

A minute later, Dr. Waldo's pocket started to ring.

He pulled out a phone, just like the one he'd given Parallel Charlie. "You arrived safely? You're sure it's your Earth? Well that's fantastic, young man! Now you be good, stay in touch, come visit, I do love visitors, you take care now! All right, goodbye, goodbye!"

That night, Charlie and Emma borrowed Ed's truck again and went back to the camping spot they now considered their own. In Earth time, they'd been there only a few days ago, but it felt like a lifetime.

"Do you think Eve will find her mother?" said Charlie, lying on a pile of thick blankets, pillows, and sleeping bags in the bed of the truck.

"I don't know. I hope so," said Emma, lying on her back next to him, gazing at the darkening sky and the stars that were just starting to twinkle in the darkness, wondering what all might be out there. She'd seen so much, and yet relatively speaking, she'd seen next to nothing. There was not just one universe to be explored, but infinite universes. Her mind couldn't help but wander, and wonder.

"I hope we can come back here next summer," said Charlie. "Not just for the lighthouse, but because I like it here."

"Me too," said Emma. Ben had called her after they'd all said goodbye to Parallel Charlie, after she and Charlie had returned to the cabin. He'd started by talking about how he, too, hoped to do more work with Dr. Waldo and the other scientists in the Hub, and ended by asking if she might like to join him for a movie night down at Wishing Rock, his town. She'd said yes, and had been glowing ever since. But more than that, she felt drawn to the Hub. Doethine had said that the elevator had found her because it wanted to be found. Emma felt the same way about the Hub. Dr. Waldo never did ask her to help, not yet anyway, and she knew the Hub wasn't hers, and yet ...

She stared up at the stars. She could never remember the constellations, so she started connecting the dots into her own configurations. "Look," she said, pointing at a pattern of stars. "It looks like Rupert."

Charlie laughed.

Emma's phone rang. Caller ID identified the caller: the Hub.

"Emma, come quick, I need you!" said an excited but breathless Dr. Waldo on the other end.

Emma looked at Charlie and grinned.

"Dr. Waldo, we are on our way!"

The adventure continues...

More aliens, more universes, more planets, more adventures!

Don't miss the thrilling continuation of the adventures of Emma, Charlie, Ben, Eve, Dr. Waldo, and all the rest, in Balky Point Adventures #2, *The Secret of the Dark Galaxy Stone*, and #3, *The Planet of the Memory Thieves*! Available in print and ebook now!

connect

If you loved *The Universes Inside the Lighthouse,* tell your friends and let Pam know! Leave a review online, send a tweet to @pamstucky, and/or drop Pam a note at facebook.com/pamstuckyauthor. Thank you!

Don't miss the second book in the series, *The Secret of the Dark Galaxy Stone!* Teens Emma and Charlie have returned to Balky Point for their winter break, and are reunited with friends Eve and Ben. This time the group is unraveling clues on their quest to find Eve's mother, but first they must track down Dr. Waldo, who has mysteriously gone missing. Their travels once again take them to far-flung places, from the other side of the Earth, to another ghost planet, to a world filled with beings they could not have imagined. Meanwhile, Emma is troubled by news that her method of travel in the past may have threatened her life, and is confronted with revelations of what lies in her future.

Visit pamstucky.com to sign up for Pam's mailing list and find out more about Pam and her other fiction and non-fiction books.

acknowledgments

It takes a village to write a book—or at least to aid and support the writer as she writes it.

Writing about the universe(s) meant I needed a pro to turn to for some space-related questions. Much gratitude to Thomas Vaughan (and his PhD in Physics) for his knowledge of all things space, because even though I don't expect to be able to construct a world that is scientifically likely, I wanted to at least try to create worlds that were scientifically possible. Thank you, Thomas, for willingly sharing your knowledge on planets, suns, habitable zones, and more.

And, when I create new worlds, that means the planets (the major ones, anyway) need names! Thank you to Samantha Stucky (a fellow list-maker) for brainstorming and helping me come up with a name for the planet Lero.

People ask all the time about my writing habits. Most often I write at home or at the library, but when I really need to get inspired and give my story a big push … I head to Happy Hour at Arnie's in Edmonds. Thank you to Christian Johnson (maker of the best lemon drops anywhere), Cynthia Bieneasz, Tina Nadeau, Vanessa Tripp, and all the rest at Arnie's for so kindly and graciously indulging me as I sit at the table in the corner, stare out at the waterfront, and write.

Thank you to the tremendously talented duo of Ken Schrag and Yasuko Nakamura for creating my cover artwork. Ken and Yasuko are multitalented artists, with a specialty in letterpress. Check out their work at www.benjaminpaul.net.

An enormous thank you to Beth Stucky, Susan Dunn, Danae Powers, Damian McGinty, and Lisa Sivertson for reading partial or full early drafts of this story. Your input, wisdom, comments, ideas, and encouragement are priceless.

Additionally, I am grateful to theoretical physicist and string theorist Brian Greene for positing multiverses. If you're interested in hearing his thoughts, check out his interview with Radiolab, "The (Multi) Universe(s)," dated Tuesday, August 12, 2008: http://www.radiolab.org/story/91859-the-multi-universes/.

Some of the ideas in this book about shame and loneliness have been inspired or enhanced by the work of Dr. Brené Brown. I highly recommend all her books and am grateful for her insights.

And, of course, thank you to the fabulous, generous, thoughtful, wonderful multitudes of people who encourage and believe in me, all along the journey. We are not alone.

Made in the USA
Monee, IL
11 April 2020